William Howe Cuyler Hosmer

**Later Lays and Lyrics**

William Howe Cuyler Hosmer

**Later Lays and Lyrics**

ISBN/EAN: 9783744787161

Printed in Europe, USA, Canada, Australia, Japan

Cover: Foto ©Andreas Hilbeck / pixelio.de

More available books at **www.hansebooks.com**

# LATER

# LAYS AND LYRICS

BY

## W. H. C. HOSMER,

AUTHOR OF

YONNONDIO, THE MONTHS, LEGENDS OF THE SENECAS,
BIRD-NOTES, ETC.

ROCHESTER, N. Y.
D. M. DEWEY,
1873.

# CONTENTS.

## BITTER MEMORIES.

## CYPRESS LEAVES.

## SONGS AND BALLADS.

## SONNET DEDICATORY.

---

BY PERMISSION OF D. M. D.

---

Friend of the poet ! after silence long,
And sad experience in the war of life—
Scattered his household gods, and worn with strife
He brings fresh offerings from the land of song.
Love for the Valley of the Genesee,
Of old the red man's favorite domain
Inspired in youth a high heroic strain
That found a generous publisher in thee.
Thy words of kind encouragement and praise
After the lapse of many weary years,
Ring like remembered music in his ears,
And back throng visions of romantic days :—
Oh ! blame him not if memory summon tears
While he inscribes to thee his "Later Lays."

W. H. C. B

Dated ROSE LAWN, AVON,
July 12th, 1872.

# QUEEN OF THE BLOSSOMS.

There was strife among the lilies,
   While throbbed each nectared cell;
There was strife among the roses,
   Each claimed to be the belle;
The winds that came to woo them
   Loved all of them so well,
They could not, with their airy tongues,
   Who was the queenliest tell.

But Onnolee, the cherub,
   Arrayed in purest white,
Burst, like a heavenly vision,
   Upon the raptured sight;
Her cheeks outblushed the roses,
   The lilies were less bright;
Her eyes like stars when cloudless
   Is June's delicious night.

Sylphs of the laughing summer
   Danced near her on the green—
The bob-o'-link and oriole,
   With breast of golden sheen;
And flashing by, with Iris dyes,
   The humming-birds were seen,
While every blossom found a tongue,
   And cried—"Behold our queen!"

# LATER LAYS.

# AGRICULTURAL ODE.

### I.

MOTHER of Arts ! that tilleth soil
　　On prairie wide, and upland lea
" Thy mercies, corn and wine, and oil,"
　　The tribes of men receive from thee.

### II.

Towns that are dotting ocean's shore,
　　The mountain-slope, and inland vale,
Could flourish populous no more,
　　If thy full granaries should fail.

### III.

States would decay ; no longer thrive
　　If God withheld .thy. golden shower ;
And nations that wax great derive
　　From thee the sinews of their power.

### IV.

Not gold alone : for those that make
　　The desert blossom like the rose
Are first Oppression's yoke to break,
　　And with proud Wrong in conflict close.

### V.

Roused like the wintry storm when bow
　　The kingly oaks beneath its might,
Our rustic fathers left the plow,
　　And met on Bunker's awful height.

VI.

While sternly marshalled there in arms,
    To drive the fell invader back,
Love for their families and farms
    Nerved them to brave the fierce attack.

VII.

A "*maranatha*" on the foe
    Their musketry in thunder pealed,
While ranks in crimson swaths lay low,
    And battle's cloud the sun concealed.

VIII.

Their deeds on that momentous day,
    In lines of light are written down
To cheer our race when thrown away,
    Like toys, are mitre, crosier, crown.

IX.

When Freedom in the mart is found
    The phantom of a sounding name,
Nursed by bold tillers of the ground
    Is a pure, patriotic flame.

X.

For them is traced a liberal creed
    In Nature's everlasting tome,
And " books in running brooks " they read
    That knit their hearts to hearth and home.

XI.

Old Art of Husbandry ! that gave
    To mortals occupation first,
Thy ministry alone could save
    When fearfully the land was cursed.

### XII.

Gray Eld, and wives and little ones
  Within the tents of Peace were fed,
When earned by sweat-drops of thy sons,
  Was man's primeval blessing—*bread*.

### XIII.

Sad exiles from their garden fair,
  While flashed behind the flaming sword,
Our great First Parents did not dare
  To dream of Paradise restored.

### XIV.

But Earth can boast of many a spot
  Redeemed by industry and skill
From wastes where roses harbored not,
  That have a smile of Eden still.

### XV.

Grenada, in romantic Spain,
  Was prosperous under Moorish sway ;
Rude hill side, and the barren plain
  Soon wore the livery of May.

### XVI.

Great Abderahmen, famed in song,
  And styled "*magnificent,*" would toil
Where golden Darro rolled along
  Laving the renovated soil.

### XVII.

Well sung the laureled bards of Rome,
  That rural life promoted health,
And Ceres, Queen of Harvest-Home,
  Was mother of the God of Wealth.

### XVIII.

Her countless banks will never fail,
   Their bases Earth from whence we sprung,
And Commerce to the salt-sea gale
   At her command the flag outflung.

### XIX.

Far from the city's stifling heat
   Chief, poet, orator and sage
To rural villas would retreat,
   And delve in Rome's Augustan Age.

### XX.

There, like the singing Lark of Ayr,
   The plow great master spirits held,
Drank rapture from the scenery fair,
   And founts that at their feet outwelled.

### XXI.

There Maro wooed, enwreathed with bays,
   The Rural Muse with art divine,
And Flaccus warbled lyric lays
   Rich as his own Falernian wine.

### XXII.

There Cincinnatus threw aside
   His rustic garb, and drew the blade
When rolled the Volscian battle tide,
   And Conscript Fathers sat dismayed ;

### XXIII.

And then in his triumphal hour,
   When the good fight was fought and won,
Resigned was dictatorial power
   By Glory's memorable son.

### XXIV.

The Guardian of a rescued land
  Found quiet on Mount Vernon's farm
When sheathed his conquering battle-brand,
  And hushed the drum-beat of alarm.

### XXV.

Alas ! that fratricidal blood
  Pollutes the land that holds his bones,
While, sitting by Potomac's flood,
  The Genius of Columbia moans !

### XXVI.

With Labor's moisture on the brow
  Kings turned the globe, once Israel's own,
And on Elijah, at the plow,
  The mantle of the Seer was thrown.

### XXVII.

What story of the Golden Age,
  In tenderness, descriptive truth,
Compares with that inspired page
  That tells us of the gleaner—Ruth ?

### XXVIII.

And imagery that most delights,
  The Past unfolding to our view,
The Royal Bard from rural sights,
  And pastoral scenes of beauty drew.

### XXIX.

" The cattle on a thousand hills "
  In Palestine we see again ;
Chime with his verse the singing rills,
  " The early, and the latter rain."

### XXX.

Theme for his minstrelsy divine
  Were brooks through fertile field that ran
" The bread that strengthens, and the wine
  That maketh glad the heart of man."

### XXXI.

In cities where the mildewed den
  Of Want yawns near the halls of Pride
Are cradeled not illustrious men
  To duty true, in danger tried.

### XXXII.

In haunts remote from scenes like these
  Are nobler spirits nursed, that tower
Like pines above the smaller trees,
  Unwarped by creed, unspoiled by power.

### XXXIII.

Far from the tumult of the town
  Loved mighty Webster to retire,
And seek, forgetful of renown,
  Fields where he labored with his sire :

### XXXIV.

Or, freed from care, he loved to dwell
  At Marshfield, by the sounding main,
Where low of kine and pastoral bell
  Disposed to calm his troubled brain.

### XXXV.

And Clay, in country costume drest,
  Sick of Corruption's wild misrule,
On his plantation in the West,
  Felt like an urchin loosed from school :

### XXXVI.

And Wright, stern Cato of the State,
   Whose honored grave is holy ground,
Towered in the Hall of high debate,
   With face and hands by toil embrowned.

### XXXVII.

Well were these famous men aware
   That impulse Agriculture gave,
To human progress everywhere,
   On solid land and rolling wave.

### XXXVIII.

The bellows would no longer blow,
   The hammer clash, the anvil ring,
If Culture should forget to sow,
   And reap the promise of the spring.

### XXXIX.

Invention baffled would despond,
   Cease progress in Mechanic·Art,
And Genius drop the wizard wand
   That governs thought, controls the heart.

### XL.

Ships would lie rotting in the bay,
   In thoroughfares the grass upgrow,
And, lords of mansions in decay,
   Reign Famine, Pestilence and Woe.

### XLI.

What spectacle more dread is found
   From Polar regions to the Line,
Than minds inactive and unsound,
   In frames of premature decline.

### XLII.

Mother of Learning—Labor Free !
     If ripens into fruit the flower,
Such ruins here he will not see,
     But grandest types of human power :—

### XLIII.

And, here, proud nursery of men !
     While rivers flow and mountains stand,
May issues of the tongue and pen
     Keep pace with issues of the hand.

## A DREAM OF THE SEA.

### I.

Stella ! while sleeping, I beheld the sea,
     Raging and heaving with convulsive throes,
Unveil its depths and mysteries to me :—
     The rock of coral like a peak arose,
Whose summit in the purple twilight glows :—
     So startling were the echoes of the caves,
Within each vein the ruddy current froze—
     The fearful conflict of the winds and waves
Methought awoke the dead in their forgotten graves

## II.

The firmament was darkened like a pall,
    And wore a look of terrible despair ;
The nymph of ocean left her sparry hall,
    And wildly shook her green, unbraided hair.
Unearthly music floated on the air
    In pauses of the storm, a dirge-like sound !
The blue shark glided from his watery lair,
    Gorged with a meal upon the ghastly drowned,
And pathway by his side the fearful sword-fish found.

## III.

Mine eye beheld forgotten works of Art,
    And heaps of gleaming perils and yellow ore ;
The costly exports of the busy mart,
    And wealth untold bestrewed old Ocean's floor :
Where were the barks that all these treasures bore ?
    Around they lay bereft of mast and sail,
To ride the deep in majesty no more—
    Defiance bidding to the angry gale,
While timid stand the brave, the manly cheeks grow
      pale.

## IV.

The fierce and huge leviathan, methought,
    Affrighted by the elemental war,
With flashing fin the upper waters sought ;
    To light the scene shot forth no twinkling star,
Nor did the bright sun in his flaming car
    On the roused deep his burning glances throw :
Black thunder clouds growled loudly, and the glare
    Of red winged lightning to the crumbling snow
That capt the surges gave intolerable glow.

### V.

Beneath the tide were visible far down
   The fallen thrones and palaces of old ;
Symbol of buried power, and ancient crown
   A skull encircled with its tarnished gold :
The wave-washed relics of the wise and bold
   In many a hollow cavern lay unwept,
And darkly hid within the tarry fold
   The hapless maid and youthful lover slept,
While over them the sea like some proud victor swept

### VI.

Spars, riven timbers, and the broken mast
   The tide retreating left upon the strand ;
Then at my feet inrolling waters cast
   My wife—the sea weed in her rigid hand :
Methought her grave I dug within the sand,
   Shrouding the precious relics in my cloak,
But when to view were lost those features bland,
   In mournful tone the passing spirit spoke—
" *Farewell for evermore !* "—I trembled and awoke

NEW YORK, 1855.

---

### THE TWO GATES.

Open in this world of sin,
Are two gates to enter in ;
Scenes unknown to mortal view,
Greet the pilgrim passing through.

One, the ivory gate of dreams,
Glows with rich, Elysian gleams ;
But more lustrous to behold,
Is the other gate of gold.
When the honey-dew of rest,
Falls upon the troubled breast,
Through the former, open wide,
Oh ! how sweet in soul to glide !
O'er its threshold, as we pass,
Seen, as in Agrippa's glass,
Are the dead of long-ago,
Moving in procession slow.
Clearly are their forms defined
Round us are their arms entwined,
And the heart, long, sad rejoices,
Hearing old, familiar voices.
Wandering, there, the soul explores
Picturesque, enchanted shores ;
Halls of fantasy where reign
Kings, discrowned on earth, again.
Dried would be a fount of bliss,
I'll be borne a world like this,
Should the pilgrim seek in vain
Entrance through that gate to gain,
Brighter than sun, moon or star,
Stands the golden gate ajar ;
Through it, to the Angel-Land,
Love and faith walk hand in hand.
Fount of its effulgent blaze,
Is the " Ancient One of Days ! "
And a host of minstrels crowned,
Flood celestial air with sound.

Those who enter in, no more
Sorrow on Time's crumbling shore—
Lost to us although we yearn,
Months and years, for their return.
Thither go, when done with life,
Mother fond, and faithful wife ;
Children laid in earth with tears,
Martyred saints and holy seers.
War, in that unclouded realm,
Never dons his brazen helm ;
Evil, there erects no throne—
Sorrow is a name unknown.
Would ye seek the blossoms lost,
In this land of killing frost,
For the pilgrimage prepare,
Morn and eve with contrite prayer.
To the clime of Endless Morn,
Hope not, man or woman born,
Passage, with corrupted mind,
Through the Golden Gate to find.

---

## SPIRIT INTERVIEWS.

### I.

FAIR as a lunar bow that queenly night,
  When loveliest around her starry brow
Twines, while the fairies dance in their delight,
  Art thou, art thou.

## II.

Remote a sweet, enchanted region lies
  From this discordant world where mortals pine,
And my glad spirit thither nightly flies
  To meet with thine.

## III.

A magic stairway to a turret leads,
  Where we look forth on Beauty's chosen home ;
Green lawns and lakelets edged with golden reeds,
  And amber foam.

## IV.

From a rich oriel window we command
  A view more fair than ever gladdened seer,
And brighter far than Beulah's lovely land
  To Christian dear.

## V.

Crowned with resplendent battlements and towers,
  We see the hills of endless summer rise ;
From base to summit carpeted with flowers
  Of Iris dyes.

## VI.

In pauses of our colloquy, unheard
  By mortal ear, awake melodious bands,
As if the harps of Paradise were stirred
  By countless hands.

## VII.

In that weird realm two souls that throb as one
  Need not bethrothal ring, nor nuptial rite,
Their bridal robes by airy beings spun
  Of bloom and light.

VIII.

How dim the Greek's Elysium, with its bowers,
  Contrasted with love's Eden where I stroll,
With Caledonian Mary gathering flowers
  Soul knit to soul !

---

## MARCH VIEW FROM HILLSIDE.

THE air is chill—the lake lies spread
Paler than shroud that wraps the dead ;
Save its mid-current, blue as steel,
While spray drops whiten, and congeal.
Oh ! how unlike its summer dress,
A sheet of azure loveliness,
In which the swallow dips his wings,
And breaks its breast, in rippling rings,
When the scared water-fowl upsprings !
The trees along its frozen shore
Wear not the look in June they wore,
Flinging deep shade the greensward o'er,
With leaf harps trembling when the breeze
To music woke their emerald keys.

Conesus ! in my younger days
I looked on gently sloping farms,
Rich frame-work for thy silvery charms,
With fixed, enamored gaze ;

Sails gleaming on thy crystal sheet,
Glanced on the sight, and disappeared,
As if by airy phantoms steered,
And Nature woke no sound more sweet
Than the low, lulling measured beat
Of foam-flaked, undulating swells
On glittering sands inlaid with shells.

Old legends cling to lake and shore,
But they inspire my lay no more,
Though, in my younger, happier years,
While sighed the wind among the pines,
And old oaks with their clinging vines
I heard, methought, the talk of seers,
And sachems, near the " Haunted Spring,"
To listeners in the council ring ;
Or when wan moonlight flecked the waters
Would spirit barks, to fancy's eye
Filled with the greenwood's dusky daughters,
Float without oar or paddle by.

How changed the scene ! a clouded arch
Borrows no lustre from the morn,
While that wild trumpeter, young March,
Is blowing on his battle-horn.
Less dread was Winter's iron reign,
And bleak and bare lie ridge and plain,
While Hillside Farm is sad to-day
Beneath a sky of leaden gray,
For nevermore will walk as lord,
My friend upon its meadow sward,
And look upon a landscape round

In mellow Autumn unexcelled,
And dreamy,'like enchanted ground,
In Summer time beheld :
But mid these scenes, renowned in song,
His memory will be cherished long ;
For here his rural home he made,
The landscape by his presence graced,
And leaves behind to view displayed,
In wintry gloom, or summer shade,
Marks of his elegance and taste.

HILLSIDE, March 6, 1866.

## HALLOWEEN.

### I.

I HAD a vision :—in'my dream
I looked on Doon's enchanted stream,
The moonlight glinted forth its beam
      On hill, and cairn.
And one I saw who reigns supreme
      Apollo's bairn.

### II.

The bard, renowned in distant climes,
Sighed for the sports of other times
When bells rang out their merry chimes,
      And lads were seen
With lassies singing quaint old rhymes
      At Halloween.

### III.

" These customs of an elder day,"
He said, " should never pass away,
Till flowers should wreath the pole in May,
      And on the green
Nymphs from the Doon, and Ayr and Tay
      Should choose their Queen.

### IV.

" Hearts, leal and warm, old manners hail !
Braw lads in Caledon will fail
When, as the evening shades prevail,
      No more are seen
Blythe lassie pulling plants of kail
      At Halloween.

### V.

" With them in soul, on sic a night,
Your minstrel, Burns, still takes delight,
And though unseen by mortal light,
      His spirit glance
Sees on the lawn, with moonshine bright,
      The fairies dance.

### VI.

" At ingle-neuks on every farm
Let witch and warlock wake alarm,
The burning nuts still work a charm
      At Halloween,
So loved when arm I locked in arm
      With Bonny Jean.

### VII.

"By, on the wind while spirits pass,
Rustling the leaves and withered grass,
Still let the pale and trembling lass
        Her apple eat,
And in the haunted looking glass
        A husband greet.

### VIII.

" Indeed will Scottish hearts be cold,
Her glory like a tale that's told
When ancient rites and customs old
        Are loved no' more,
And only worshippers of gold
        Crowd Albyn's shore."

### IX.

Deep silence fell upon the place,
The poet's noble form and face,
Fled in my dream and left no trace,
        Like vanished smoke ;
I heard Doon's waves each other chase,
        And I awoke.

McPherson Lodge, Oct. 31, 1865.

## THE MARKHAM ELM.*

### I.

LIKE an old warrior with his helm,
  Decked grandly with a crest of green,
A thousand years has stood yon Elm,
  Chief glory of the scene !

### II

What tales, if its old trunk could talk,
  Would fall upon the listening ear,
Of the wild wolf upon his walk,
  The red-man with his spear.

### III.

It towered the giant of the wood,
  In a rich robe of emerald drest,
When launched upon the ocean flood,
  Columbus sought the west.

### IV.

It braved old winter's rudest shock
  When the storm-fiends their trumpets blew,
When on stern Plymouth's hallowed rock
  Landed the May-Flower's crew.

### V.

It was the forest's pride, when came
  The Norsemen, borne grey ocean o'er,
And the Round Tower, long known to fame,
  Built on New England's shore,

*This noble tree, stands on Markham Flats, near the dividing line between Avon and Rush. It is forty feet in circumference, and before it was shorn, by time, of its old protecting boughs, it shadowed an acre of ground. It was celebrated in Indian tradition, and under its capacious canopy Chief, Sage, and Warrior, met in the old time. Some wretch, who little regards what is venerable and historic, kindled a fire in its hollow boll. May the curse of the poet, and the malediction of God, rest on him forevermore !

### VI.

Behemoth, in its mighty shade,
　　Has grazed, perchance, and couched him down ;
His nest, the forest Eagle made,
　　Within its royal crown.

### VII.

Beneath its old protecting boughs,
　　Perchance have Indian lovers met
To hold sweet tryst, and pledge their vows
　　To maids with locks of jet.

### VIII.

Its branches have the Panther screened,
　　Rough with the hues, and moss of age ;
Chiefs round its Titan trunk convened,
　　Have met in council sage.

### IX.

It stands alone ;—the river near
　　Breaks, with sad whisper on the shore,
As if its waters longed to hear
　　The Indian's voice once more.

### X.

Like an old tribeless sachem now,
　　It stands dejected and alone,
And the wind, lifting up its bough,
　　Gives out a mournful moan.

### XI.

Within its hollow trunk are seen
　　The smoky, blackened marks of fire,
Though in its top of loving green
　　The wind still tunes its lyre.

XII.

And worse than Vandal, thou, who marred
　　Its bark with villainy malign ;—
The Malediction of the Bard
　　Forevermore be thine !

———————+•+———————

## NOOK OF BEAUTY.

---

*Suggested by a New Hampshire view from the gifted pencil*
*of W. H. Hilliard.*

---

I.

HERE is a lovely scene,
A nook of summer beauty 'mid the hills,
Tuneful with wind-swept pines, and silver rills,
　　While, clothed in living green,
Are pastures where the lowing cattle graze,
And distance mellowed to a purple haze.

II.

Kine quaffing from the stream
Stand with their shadows on the water flung ;
　　A brighter summer dream
Was never sketched by Art, by poet sung ;
One, who thus dips his brush in Nature's hues,
Commands the homage of the Poet's muse.

2

### III.

Young Artist ! study well
The matchless scenery of my native vale,
Its cataracts that thunder on the gale,
 Lawn, breezy hill, and dell ;
Go where the Genesee to run his course
Leaps pure, and mountain born, with youthful force

———————◆———————

*Lines Suggested by a Tableau Vivant, representing*
## NAPOLEON CROSSING MOUNT ST. BERNARD

———

I THOUGHT that Death had swallowed in his gulf
" The mightest genius of five thousand years ;"
But there he sits upon his rearing steed,
Tall Alpine peaks before him, and behind,
His weary cohorts struggling through the snow,
And dragging up the steep dismounted guns,
Lashed firmly in rude troughs of hollowed pine.
They falter in their task-work, but the drums
Beat hurriedly the charge, and fainting forms
Change into figures of resistless power,
And fierce eyes flash, as if the foe were near.
It cannot be illusion, or the work
Of wondrous sorcery ; for, lo ! the flag—
The tri-color that flapped its glorious folds
In conquered capitals—is streaming forth
Its gorgeous splendor to the freezing blast.

Power to conceive, and will to execute,
On the great captain's face, are deeply stamped ;
And in his glance there is a gleam of joy,
As if he scorned the vale, the level plain,
And loved the home of eagles and of storms.

Henceforth I will believe the legends strange
Of wizard Merlin and Agrippa told ;
For Art a triumph has achieved to-night,
That throws in shade their most potential charms—
Snatched from the gloomy Past his iron keys,
And wove a spell that back to mortal gaze,
Summons the man of destiny once more ;
Regardless of the threatening avalanche,
By thundering torrent and the mountain gorge,
Forcing a passage to Marengo's field.

## BATTLE OF TEMPERANCE.

### 1.

THERE's a mustering of forces
   From the mountain and the glen—
Men are arming for the struggle,
   Not apologies for men.
Dry bones are to life awaking,
   And prophetic eyes behold
Wonders to the "Vale of Vision,"
   Like those grandly seen of old.

II.

Long the tribes of men have languished
   Under a destroying curse ;
Sore were plagues that fell on Egypt,
   But Intemperance is worse.
In its gallery of portraits,
   Lighted by the fires of Hell,
Flame out faces of the fallen,
   Painted fearfully and well.

III.

Lo ! the heads of mighty genius
   In dark frames arrest the gaze !
Round each broad, Byronic forehead
   Serpents intertwined with bays.
Features of one, greatly gifted,
   There the startled eye discerns ;
Scotland's own immortal singer,
   Early marked for ruin—Burns !

IV.

Artists of divine conception
   That the pencil dropped at noon—
Poets, in their wild delirium,
   Waking harp-strings out of tune ;
And a face of kingly splendor,
   With unutterable woe
Stamped on all its lines of beauty,
   Whispers to the gazer—Poe !

V.

Sovereigns robed in royal purple
   In that gallery are seen—

Loathsome marks of dissipation
   Blotting out majestic mien.
Alexander, crushing nations
   Underneath his iron heel,
Outlined with the blood of Clytus
   Clinging to his ruthless steel :

### VI.

And the mighty king, Belshazzar !
   Drunken in his festal hall,
While a pencil, tipped with lightning,
   Writes his doom upon the wall :
And the "scourge of God" who perished
   When a thousand fields were won,
Overthrown by wine, the mocker,
   Attila, the royal Hun.

### VII.

In that gallery of horror
   Darker sights the vision pain,
Truth's apostles by the Demon
   Of destroying habit slain :
Priests, ordained of God, that yielded
   When "the still small voice" was dumb,
An inheritance in heaven
   Madly bartering for rum.

### VIII.

Count the raindrops that are swallowed
   By the vast, engulphing main,
Not the victims by this agent
   Of the Powers of Darkness slain.

Pestilence that walks at midnight,
   War that reddens land and sea,
Monster ! born of distillation,
   Are but dwarfs compared to thee.

### IX.

By no lines the realm is bounded
   O'er which Alcohol, the king,
Holds his reign of death and terror
   While the birds of hope take wing.
Based on God-like mind in ruin,
   On Love's bleeding, broken heart,
Is his throne, from which the Furies
   On their fearful mission start.

### X.

Who asks where his court is holden?
   With his satraps, Death, Despair,
In the churchyard and the dungeon,
   On the scaffold—find it there !
Find it where poor widowed mourners
   For their starving orphans wail,
And a host of homeless vagrants
   Crowd the poor-house and the jail.

### XI.

Where the druggist sells his bitters,
   Though it works the people ill,
And beneath a lying label
   Hides the serpent of the still:
Where ten thousand homes, once happy,
   By the sheriff have been sold,
Bought by venders of the poison,
   Blood on their ill-gotten gold.

### XII.

Live we in a land of Freedom,
  While a countless host of slaves,
Bone and sinew of the country,
  Stagger to dishonored graves?
While the Senate is polluted
  By inebriates void of shame,
Faithless to high trusts confided,
  Blots upon the Nation's fame?

### XIII.

Band, my brothers! for the conflict,
  Though it prove a weary strife,
And, beneath our Temple's banner,
  In God's name enlist for life.
Let the torrent of Destruction
  Be arrested in its flow,
Bearing to a gulf of darkness
  Rich and poor, the high and low.

---

## WINTEMOYEH.

### I.

WINTEMOYEH! Wintemoyeh!
  Fairest of the forest daughters!
Still thy voice of lamentation
  Rises from the silver waters.
Well I love yon lake of beauty
  Cradled amid mountains green,
For a sad, and olden legend,
  Links thy memory to the scene.

### II.

Wintemoyeh ! Wintemoyeh !
  Dark and dreary was the day
When the bravest of my tribesmen
  Fell in battle far away.
By the crafty Sioux surrounded
  On the prairies of the West,
Long they waged unequal conflict,
  Foot to foot, and breast to breast.

### III.

Washed away are stains of battle
  By the rains of long ago,
And tall grasses, rankly growing,
  Hide old bones that bleach below.
There unburied lies thy lover,
  In his strength and pride cut down—
Vain his love for Wintemoyeh,
  Vain his longings for renown.

### IV.

When a runner of her people
  Brought the fearful tidings back
To her wild, distempered vision,
  As the midnight morn grew black.
To a rocky platform jutting
  From the wooded mountain side,
When the summer day was dying
  Crazed, young Wintemoyeh hied.

### V.

Far below, with softened murmur,
  Curled the billows up the beach,

And the silence oft was broken
  By the lone owl's boding screech ;
But she cared not for the hooting
  Of dull night's ill-omened bird,
While her black, dishevelled tresses
  By the evening wind was stirred.

### VI.

From her breast the silver broaches
  Rudely with her hand she tore—
From her soft arms pulled the bracelets,
  For their brightness charméd no more,
Then with wailing cadence floated
  Her sad death-song on the air,
And the music was in keeping
  With her look of wild despair.

### VII.

Followed fast her friends to save her,
  But she heeded not their cries ;
Looked her last upon the mountains,
  And the purple sunset skies ;
Madly calling on her lover,
  Then she took the desperate leap,
And the Swan Lake gave her burial
  In its hollows dark and deep.

### VIII.

Wintemoyeh ! Wintemoyeh !
  Fairest of the forest daughters !
Still thy voice of lamentation
  Rises from the silver waters ;

And the hunter, home-returning
   At the hush of twilight gray,
Sees a phantom, in the distance,
   On the billows melt away.

---

## JUNE DYING.

### I.

In crimson flakes on the garden mould,
   Are the fallen rose-leaves lying,
And the mystic wind, that harper old,
   Through my ravaged bower is sighing
         A low, sad tune,
         For beautiful June
            Is dying.

### II.

The whistle clear of the mother quail
   To the mead lark is replying,
And airy tongues in wood and dale,
   Sweet, many-voiced are crying
         " Too soon, too soon
         Our beautiful June
            Is dying."

### III.

With saddened note o'er the faded lawn
  The barn-swallow low is flying;
A youthful bloom from the land is gone,
  For the "Strawberry Moon" is dying,
      And the crickets croon
      That beautiful June
      Is dying.

### IV.

Dry summer dust that veils its green,
  Through the village park is flying,
And cloudy forms on the wing are seen
  To Beauty's death-bed hieing,
      For that peerless boon
      Of our Maker, June,
      Is dying.

## FLORAL GIFTS.

### I.

Thanks, lady ! for these beauteous flowers
Bright with the diamonds of the showers:
The deep, clear blue of summer skies
Mingles its tints with other dyes :
The first, faint blush of waking day
Gives to the pink its rich array,
And honey-suckle cups unfold
Inlaid with sunset's richest gold.

### II.

But why the storied poppy bring
To crown this floral offering?
Old poets in the lap of Dis
Have flung a strange weird flower like this;
Called it the Rose of Proserpine
Filled with a dread, Plutonian wine:
Its scent disposes one to rest
On the green turf, our mother's breast.

### III.

Of all that grace the bright bouquet
The poppy I will choose to-day;
No flower, that memory wakes, for me!
While my heart pulses like a sea
On which lorn wrecks are drifting past,
No ground for Hope to anchor fast:
The wondrous plant from which distils
Forgetfulness can cure all ills.

### IV.

I would forget that friends grow cold,
That Beauty groweth dim and old;
I would forget that woman's faith
Is frail, and never kept till death;
That one long loved hath proven false,
A butterfly to flirt and waltz;
Inconstant as the treacherous sand
When wooing billows kiss the strand.

### V.

Then, lady! thanks in this dark hour,
For hushed oblivion's chosen flower;

It drowsy influence will cure
Sharp agonies I ill endure ;
Better than joy's blue myrtle crown,
Better than laurel of renown
When one is tired of life and light
Is the dark poppy, born of night ;
God's words are on each leaf imprest
" He giveth his beloved rest."

## SUMMER RAIN.

### I.

What sound so sweet,
After a day of fiery heat,
And sunstrokes in the dusty street,
As the pleasant voice of the singing rain
Dashing against the window pane.

### II.

The queenly rose,
And vassal flowers their eyes unclose,
While God his benison bestows ;
And the sick man dreams of health again
Cheered by the dance of the dropping rain.

### III.

The bubbles break,
While showers descend on the breezy lake,
And the water nymphs from slumber wake.
Homeward driving his harvest wain
The farmer curses the cooling rain!

### IV.

The plague fiend stops
In his dread career to hear the drops;
Then, farmer! why mourn o'er your crops?
True faith sublime ne'er leaned in vain
On the Power that sends us the healing rain.

### V.

It bringeth cure
To the blistered feet of the starving poor,
And their hearts are strengthened to endure;
While wo, in love with life again,
His hot brow bares to the welcome rain.

### VI.

Of murmuring shells,
And the silvery chime of fairy bells,
Were never born such music spells,
To cheer the visionary brain
Of listening bard as the summer rain.

### VII.

Earth looks more fair
When drops that banish the sun's hot glare
Fall from the cisterns of upper air;
And her breast is cleansed of many a stain
By the gentle bath of the summer rain.

### VIII.

It caught its chime,
Not in this fading realm of time,
But above, above in a holier clime;
And I ever hear an angel's strain
Blend with the dash of the summer rain.

———•••———

## SEPTEMBER IDYL.

———

" The sultry summer past, September comes—
Soft twilight of the slow declining year."—[CARLOS WILCOX.]

———

### I.

Light gossamer by fairies spun,
   And thistle stars are changed to gold,
Where rich autumnal bursts of sun
    Light up the forests old:
In my lost youth these ancient oaks
Gave shelter with their emerald cloaks,
And friends they seem, by years unchanged,
Though others have been long estranged.

### II.

Here watch in boyhood's day I kept,
   My game-bag filled with feathered spoil,
And phantoms rise, that long have slept,
    From legendary soil.

Lo ! tameless hunters of the deer,
Bearing their antlered prey, draw near—
Tall shapes of Apollonian grace,
With *Freedom* written on each face.

### III.

By Uhland seen were spirits twain,
   That with him crossed the haunted waves,
And back the long deplored again
      Come from forgotten graves.
Disturbing not the slumbering ferns,
My first love, and my last, returns,
Her dark eye flashing with the light
Of day-break through its depths of night.

### IV.

Gay butterflies, in saffron clad,
   On places moist with rain alight,
Though carpeted with vesture sad
      Are glades with bloom once bright.
White frost that made the herbage sere
Has purified our atmosphere,
And o'er the breezy world is thrown
A charm to summer-time unknown.

### V.

While other birds, too sad for song,
   In longer flight their pinions try,
The migratory black-birds throng
      And pipe a blithe good-bye!
Wild fife-notes, tremulous and shrill,
Prove that the mead-lark lingers still,
And guardian of her brood from foes,
The quail a signal-whistle blows.

## VI.

Some prowling fox must be astir,
  For flushed in hazel coppice near
The ruffed-grouse, with tumultuous whirr,
    Speeds by on wing of fear.
Sure of a flying mark no more,
Though deadly was mine aim of yore,
The creature now is far away,
And cover close will keep to-day.

## VII.

The hen-hawk with a hungry scream
  Mounts up in widening rings of flight,
Edged its broad pinions with a gleam
    Of mellowed amber light.
From floral cups and bells the bee
Bears nectar to the hollow tree,
While the shrill locust wakes a lay
That tells of summer passed away.

## VIII.

This nook of loveliness I sought
  In many sylvan tramp of yore—
The happy heart that then I brought
    Beats in this breast no more.
While ambushed, where the woods set bounds
To yellow, grainy stubble-grounds,
I listen to the pigeon's coo,
And rush of plumage darkly blue.

## IX.

Although in reach of leaden showers
  The hungry flock are settling down

Thought wanders back to other hours,
   And visions of renown :
Well may the Manton by my side
Be hushed, its deadly force untried,
For quaffs my soul celestial wine,
And golden reveries are mine.

---

## NOVEMBER.

### I.

I hear the wail of the pitiless gale
   Round the couch of Beauty dying,
And deep in tone as the hoarse trombone
   Are the calls of the wild geese flying :
While wanes the year how lone and and drear
   Is the heart of the minstrel feeling,
For the voiceful blast that is hurrying past
   Is the dirge of autumn pealing.

### II.

Where field flowers sprang and bird-notes rang
   The rude gale pipes a warning ;
By vapors dun that hide the sun,
   Festooned are the halls of morning.
Hail, rain and storm of colors warm
   Have robbed the woodlands faded
That wore of late, in royal state,
   Tints born of the rainbow braided.

### III.

When day is o'er clouds deck no more
  The west with their golden fleeces,
And purple cloaks on the kingly oaks
  Are torn by the gust in pieces.
A crimson glow on the sward below
  Of late were the maples flinging,
But boughs are bare in the freezing air
  On which the crows are swinging.

### IV.

In what fair isle of tropical smile
  Is the bright Indian summer staying?
Will the nymph no more to this northern shore
  Come soft with the south wind playing?
In vain we yearn for her dear return,
  She visits the land no longer;
With the tribes of old from a clime so cold
  She fled when the whites grew stronger.

## A FALL LYRIC.

### I.

Heir of Summer's crown, September!
Soon will fade thy last red ember:
Seasons come and go like waves
Subsiding into ocean caves—

Naught is enduring here :
The cup of bliss conceals alloy,
And faces, wreathed with smiles of joy,
    Mask shuddering fear,
        Passing away ! passing away !
Is writ on the hillside and the vale ;
  Flowers that blushed at the break of day,
Ere twilight-time turn pale.
What is the burthen of the song
That floats on the midnight blast along :
The words of fearful warning heard
In the voice of the rill, and the warble of bird ?
The wild refrain of the stormy lay
Roared by the cataract, night and day ?
        Passing away ! passing away !

## II.

Nought endures that finite man
    In his arrogance uprears ;
Tower and temple he may plan,
Sons complete what sires began,
    But revolving years
Arch and column undermine
Draped with the dark green ivy-twine,
And the bat and the owl flap their dismal wings,
In the desolate courts of departed kings,
And silence holds sway in baronial halls
Where the grim face of Ruin the gazer appalls.
        Passing away ! passing away !
When were words uttered so full of dismay ?
How on my heart, like a knell, they are falling,
While through the darkness sad voices are calling

" Sorrow is ever the neighbor of mirth,
Nothing is stable and constant on earth :
      Oh ! how brief !
   Winter's dazzling flake of snow,
   Vernal flowers the first to blow,
   Summer's rose, autumnal leaf."

### III.

Of little profit is wealth that we hoard,
   Place and position are worse than vain ;
Honors achieved by pen, tongue and the sword,
   Ere the goal of our hopes we gain,
Break like frail bubbles awoke by the rain—
   Chase of renown is rewarded with pain,
A heart-ache, a hungering void in the soul
That longs for escape from its mortal control,
      Passing away ! passing away !
Words only uttered by creatures of clay,
Are not inscribed on the portal of day,
Guarding approach to the beautiful shore
Washed by the stream we are ferrying o'er.
Forms on the dazzling, auriferous sands
Gather, and wave their pale, beckoning hands :
Woven of starlight are robes that they wear,
Each stately head ringed with a circlet of gold ;
One I know well by her dark, glossy hair,
A beautiful being of Phidian mould.
Oh ! I am under her wondrous control,
Melt her soft tones in the ear of my soul ;
Sprinkled with heart-drops are words of her lay
" Hither, come hither ! where wreaths never wither
And idols are turned into mouldering clay,
While Love warbles mournfully passing away ?

Bulbs that we bury shoot forth into flowers
   When resurrection accompanies spring
Giving dark green to the skeleton bowers,
   Painting the newly-born butterfly's wing,
Spirits released from their chrysalis state,
Flitting through Summerland's golden-arched gate,
Care not where lies the poor, perishing shell,
Loathsome, and dread with mortality's smell—
Enough that the bondage of earth-life is o'er,
And grief can encumber, guilt darken no more."

———————◦◆◦————— ——

## TO INDIAN RIVER.

———

### 1.

Brunette among the streams !
   The rose of sunset gleams
Like color in an Indian maiden's cheek
    Upon thy shadowed breast,
    Where wild fowl love to rest
From flight awhile when breeding haunts they seek.

### II.

When comes sweet Summer-time,
   To cheer our Northern clime,
How pleasant is a voyage along thy shore;
    Still dark with forests shades,
    While frowning palisades
Rise in rude grandeur from a rocky floor.

### III.

The fisherman delights
On calm, mid-summer nights
His skiff by torchlight quietly to steer—
A flash—a sullen plunge—
And the strong muscallonge
Receives his death-stroke from the deadly spear.

### IV

The red man's ancient trail
Is blotted from the vale,
Through which the troubled waters foam and flow,
But still his camp-fires blaze,
As in departed days,
Where Rocky Point looks down upon the waves below

### V.

At twilight hour afloat
Sped on our bonny boat,
While foam-bells sparkled, bursting in her wake,
Until she ploughed her way,
By mimic cape and bay,
To the charmed portals of a lovely lake.

### VI.

Waves by no inlet fed
In their romantic bed
Were furrowed lightly by our gliding prow ;
Trees on the rocky banks,
Arrayed in scattered ranks,
To groves, the surface under seemed to bow.

### VII.

High up, in caverned stone,
Their eyrie, dark and lone,
Fierce forest eagles made in other years ;
Still proof against the storm,
Huge nests of basket-form
The vision of the passing boatman cheers.

### VIII.

Wild dear no more to drink
From runways to the brink
Follow the stately leader of the herd,
But trapped with cunning skill
Are mink and muskrat still
Where flag and reed are by the south wind stirred

### IX

Would I could trace thy course
To its primeval source,
In wilds alone by wandering hunter sought ;
There the huge moose abides,
The savage panther hides,
And beaver-dams are marvellously wrought.

### X.

Through grander rivers flow,
With Summer's kiss aglow,
While pleasure-barges on their bosom ride,
Brunette among the streams !
The poet in his dreams
Will often float upon thy dusky tide.

## THE THOUSAND ISLES.

Air—"Beautiful Isle of the Sea."

### I.

Isles of enchantment divine !
  Glory ye give to a river
Broader than Danube or Rhine,
  Brighter than swift Gauldalquiver.
Midsummer hangs round your shores
  Mists that are purple and golden ;
Song times the dipping of oars,
  Now, as in the days that are olden.

### CHORUS.

  Haunts of the tameless and wild !
    Homes of the fearless and free !
  Lovelier isles never smiled,
    Belted by blue of the sea.

### II.

Isles that laugh first when the spring
  Frees from ice-bondage the torrents,
Jewels are ye in the ring
  Worn by the mighty St. Lawrence.
Indian encampments of yore
  Charms to the scenery were lending ;
O'er yon dark cedars no more
  Smoke from old hearths is ascending.
    Haunts of the tameless, &c.

### III.

.Isles where the morning first beams,
  More than a thousand in number,

3

Oft still I see ye in dreams,
　　Woke by the wild winds from slumber.
Channels of silvery flow
　　Gems of the sisterhood sever;
Evergreen mantles bestow
　　Beauty that drapes them forever.
　　　　　Haunts of the tameless, &c.


### IV.

Oberon, king of the elves !
　　Court in yon arbor seems holding ;
Blossoms on gray, rocky shelves,
　　Wet by the spray, are unfolding.
Undine to Echo might list,
　　Sands grained with gold for a pillow,
Where water-lillies are kissed
　　By the blue lips of the billow.
　　　　　Haunts of the tameless, &c.


### V.

Edens, bewitchingly fair !
　　Soft, crimson haze o'er ye hovers ;
Bowers giving fragrance to air,
　　Wove by the wood-nymphs for lovers.
Scarred in the battle of life,
　　Folly and falsehood forsaking,
Who would not rest from the strife,
　　Home midst these green islands making ?
　　　　　Haunts of the tameless, &c.

## VERSES FOR EASTER.

———

" The ostrich leaveth her eggs in the earth, and warmeth them in the dust
Job—xxix : 14

———

### I.

Unstudied verses let me weave,
While ring the bells of Easter Eve,
And eggs of many hues that gleam,
Gifts to the children, be my theme !

### II.

By Job, that holy man of old,
Of the wild ostrich we are told,
Who hides beneath the covering sand,
Her bright eggs in a weary land,

### III.

In grave unmarked by mortal eye,
In the mute dust, her treasures lie,
Until the desert sun imparts
A vital heat to embryo hearts.

### IV.

Globed are the coffins that confine
Th' unsheltered brood by law divine,
And after burial, all unheard
Is mourning by the mother-bird.

### V.

When her maternal task is wrought
She speeds away by instinct taught
That One who marks the sparrow's fall
Sepulchral seeds to life will call.

### VI.

Types of the resurrection morn
Rise the young birdlings, desert-born,
And, though a mother's care denied,
Eternal love will food provide.

### VII.

Thus faith consigns, in holy trust,
Her loved and lost to burial dust,
Assured, though gone the quick'ning breath
That endless life is born of death.

---

## HYMN TO THE VIRGIN.

*(Inscribed to Rev. Father O'Keefe.)*

BY W. H. C. HOSMER.

### I.

" *Salve Regina !* " immaculate Virgin !
   Here me implore, and thy pity bestow ;
Wild waves of trouble around me are surging,
   Light with thy smile the deep night of my woe.
Queen of the Saints ! hear my earnest petition,
   Mother of Jesus, conceived without sin,
Turn me aside from the road to perdition,
   Let me the fold of thy love enter in.
      *" Ave, Sanctissima "* !

II.

Angel of Mercy! for grevious transgression
　　Thorn-planted paths I am treading alone;
One hope remains—that thy blest intercession
　　Pardon may win at the foot of the throne.
Warring with fiends, oh! compassionate Mother!
　　When will the sweat of my agony cease,
Groans of my wounded heart how can I smother,
　　If I hear not thy low whisper of peace?
　　　　*" Ave, Sanctissima "!*

III.

Mary! thy name when bright angels are talking
　　Ever with holiest rapture is heard;
Air, though in darkness is Pestilence walking,
　　Purer becomes by the spell of that word.
Song, through the Halls of the Blest ever flowing,
　　Wafts thy sweet name on its billowy tide;
Faith, while a martyrdom dread undergoing,
　　Calling on thee has triumphantly died.
　　　　*" Ave, Sanctissima "!*

IV.

Wander in soul through Art's galleries olden—
　　How the great masters delight to portray
Mother and child crowned with radiance golden
　　Shaming the tamer effulgence of day.
Theme of high bard are the Loves and the Graces
　　Flocking, like birds, round their Paphian Queen
Mary and babe, with far lovelier faces,
　　Eyes of my spirit in visions have seen.
　　　　*" Ave, Sanctissima "!*

V.

Bearing my cross the dread burden grows lighter
  "*Ave, Maria*"*!* peals out on the air;
Darkness is fleeing, the prospect grows brighter,
  While hope bridges over the gulf of despair.
Mother of God! guard Earth's motherless daughters,
  Teach them to bend willing knee at thy shrine;
Pilot them over the perilous waters,
  Guide them, at last, to a haven divine.
    "*Ave, Sanctissima*"*!*

VI.

All through Eve lost was be Mary recovered,
  Pearl of the Sisterhood! free from all guilt;
Bloom follows blight where her spirit hath hovered,
  Wonders are wrought where her alters are built.
Fair is the lily, but Mary is fairer,
  O'er my heart's realm may she reign without end;
Tender and true is the love that I bear her,
  Knightly my zeal her pure sway to extend.
    "*Ave, Sanctissima*"*!*

## GOD'S TENT.

I.

LET every knee be bent,
  Let every head be bowed,
For in this holy tent
  Speaks Deity aloud.

The islands and the lands
   In loved embrace it holds,
Not made with human hands
   Are its blue curtain folds.

II

A countless host encamps
   Within, watched o'er by Love ;
Sun, moon and stars are lamps
   That light it from above.
These things endowed with breath,
   Pour out perpetual praise,
And Life's pale sister, Death,
   Clasped hands at times will raise.

III.

What stirs devotion deep
   Like voices that arise
When Nature wakes from sleep,
   And darkness drapes the skies—
When tribes of earth are dumb,
   And storm unfurls its wings,
While thunder beats his drum,
   And bass roused Ocean sings ?

IV.

By billow, breeze and bird
   A ritual is read
Sweeter than written word
   By priest or abbot said.
Hymns sung by falling showers
   Beyond the reach of art,
Those smiles of God, the flowers,
   Rebuke a thankless heart.

### V.

Shall man no praise bestow,
　A prayerless mute be seen
While thanks the cattle low
　To God for pastures green—
While mountains that aspire
　His majesty proclaim,
And clouds have tongues of fire
　That thunder out his name?

### VI.

Grand are the waves of sound
　That through old minsters roll,
　Stirring the heart's profound,
Lifting on high the soul;
　But in God's holy tent
Is grander music far,
　Its dome, the firmanent,
Its lamps, sun, moon and star.

## MOUNT OF VISION.

### I.

Stand on the charmed Mount of Vision with me
　Washed by a river that glimmers below;
Crowning its headlands a city I see,
　Turret and tower with the morning aglow.

Palm groves give shade to suburban retreats,
   Ruby and sapphire flash out from the walls,
Lovely are shapes in the pearl-paven streets,
   Saintly are heads that look forth from its halls.

### II.

Music I hear that sad hearts have desired
   Sending electrical life through the veins;
Mighty, old masters, when rapt and inspired,
   Never could waken such exquisite strains.
How limn with pencil a picture so fair,
   Paint in weak colors the Land of the Blest;
Hill-slopes that purple of royalty wear,
   Vales in rich glow of the emerald drest!

### III.

Forms of the loved and lost gladden the sight,
   Beings of beauty deplored by me long
Wave their white hands, and I catch with delight
   Wandering notes of ecstatical song.
Come to my arms, let me clasp thee again
   Innocent child, wearing ringlets of gold!
Bride of my youth! that I mourn for in vain,
   Come with the passionate greeting of old!

### IV.

Would I had wings to flee swiftly away
   Thither where grief never uttered a moan—
Spirits relieved from the bondage of clay
   Over yon River find passage alone.
Fade into shadow those fields ever green,
   Towers, by no mortal hand built disappear;
Roseate mists drop a curtain between
   Sand-wastes of Time, and Love's holier sphere.

# WAR LYRICS.

# ANNUS MIRABILIS.

## I.

TIME'S belfry, with another knell,
　　Is in the wintry tempest shaking,
And Ocean, with an angry swell,
　　Is on the beach in thunder breaking.
Another pilgrim reached the goal
　　When waned the last hour of December,
And left behind a blood-red scroll
　　That man will evermore remember.

## II.

To Europe for a mighty theme
　　No more in thought the bard will wander,
But here, awaking from his dream,
　　Upon the fate of empire ponder.
Of greatest moment are events
　　Within one year's brief limits crowded ;
Potomac's shore all white with tents,
　　Heroic martyrs early shrouded.

## III.

Fields with fraternal gore are red
　　Where Peace, of late, the grain was reaping ;
From rugged Maine to Hilton Head
　　Are widowed ones, and Orphans weeping.

The hardy Anglo-Saxon race
  Now, as of old, are slow to anger,
But when concession is disgrace
  They love the battle's shock and clangor.

### IV.

Departed Year! the book of Time
  Is filled with memorable pages,
Recording wars, and deeds sublime
  That scatter night from perished ages.
But, ah! not one of these can chain
  Such grand material for story
As leaf that registers thy name,
  Though sorrow mingles with the glory.

### V.

Unsparing, parracidal hands
  Have lifted steel to pierce a mother
Whose fall, in many groaning lands
  The spark of liberty would smother.
In vain have patriots implored—
  Misled by chiefs whose hearts were rotten;
Revolted states have grasped the sword,
  And every solemn oath forgotten.

### VI.

An undivided North has sworn
  This league of states shall not be broken;
Drum·beat, and blast of bugle-horn
  The marching of her hosts betoken.
Ask not, ask not, with lying mouth,
  Unblushing preacher of Disunion!
"Why should the children of the South
  With Northern mud-sills hold communion?"

### VII.

Have we no partnership in graves
   On Yorktown's plain, by Eutaw's water,
Where Britain sent her hireling slaves
   Like driven cattle to the slaughter ?
Who called New England craven when
   She fought to guard your homes and alters,
While many of the Southern men
   Grew loyal at the thought of halters ?

### VIII.

When Carolina's host had fled
   From Camden in disgraceful panic,
The chief to victory that led
   Was Greene, Rhode Island's brave mechanic.
The sword-cane and the bowie-knife
   In peaceful times we never carry ;
But strong must be the arm in strife
   That downright northern blows can parry.

### IX.

If gallant Marion from the tomb
   Could rise, how stern would be his warning,
To see the land in deeper gloom
   Than wrapped in it the nation's morning ;
To hear wild wailing in the air,
   And cries of havoc and disaster,
While tiger Slavery, in his lair,
   Crouched for the life-blood of the master.

### X.

That country never bleeds in vain
   When the dread curse of war falls on her,

Though with a hecatomb of slain
   She vindicates insulted honor.
When kind, paternal words are weak,
   And spurned the calm appeal of reason,
The cannon's iron lips must speak
   In thunder to the brood of Treason.

### XI.

The poet cherishes belief
   When nations reach the brink of ruin
Wake in their coffins sage and chief,
   To preach against the foul undoing.
Hark ! Marshfield by the sounding sea,
   And Ashland call in tones of thunder—
"This mighty Empire of the Free
   Rebellion must not rend asunder."

### XII.

Mount Vernon finds a voice, and cries
   In tones of earnest supplication,
" Ye madmen, sever not the ties
   Of fealty that States owe the Nation."
The Hermitage has vocal grown
   While near the storm of battle gathers—
"Strike ! for the soil that freemen own,
   Strike for the grave-mounds of your fathers."

### XIII.

Weep, Genius of Columbia, weep !
   With proud, but bitter drops of sorrow,
Where Winthrop and Young Ellsworth sleep
   The slumber that will know no morrow.

Like Bayard whose undimmed renown
    Gleams like a cloudless star full brightly,
Or Sydney of the laurel crown,
    They fell with harness on full knightly.

### XIV.

What land can nobler heroes boast
    Who in the van have died sublimely,
Than Lyon, Ajax of the host!
    And gallant Baker, slain untimely.
For them the marble shafts of art
    Would be a work of vain endeavor;
Their names upon the Nation's heart
    Are written, and will last forever.

### XV.

Beware of ice-bergs when afloat,
    The mighty growth of polar winters;
Or Ocean when the strongest boat
    With flail of surge he pounds to splinters.
For avalanches darkening day,
    Watch, traveler, in Alpine regions!
They have been known to sweep away
    An army with its bannered legions.

### XVI.

Volcanic fires and earthquake shock
    Mock at crowned heads and their dominions,
And deadly is the wild siroc
    Lifting the sand waste on its pinions.
Terrific, these!—but lo, a sight
    At which description lags and falters!
Armed millions rising in their might,
    And as ONE MAN to guard their alters.

### XVII.

No foreign foe pollutes our coast,
  No Vandal horde of rash invaders
To rouse in arms a grander host
  Than Hermit Peter's grim Crusaders.
Far louder than Orlando's horn
  The tocsin of alarm is ringing,
And brighter than the blaze of morn
  Our flag abroad its folds are flinging.

### XVIII.

Oh ! why should precious blood be spilled
  By rending shot and dripping sabre,
Where God has with abundance filled
  The bursting granaries of Labor ?
Give answer, vile, insurgent crew,
  More heartless far that fiends infernal,
To Country, Home and Heaven untrue,
  And doomed to infamy eternal !

### XIX.

No longer in your hellish hate,
  A hope to crush this Union cherish :
Immutable and fixed as fate
  Is the decree that Guilt must perish.
Truth's champions can know no fear,
  For love divine is watching o'er them,
And frightened by their charging cheer,
  The Powers of Darkness flee before them.

### XX.

Port Royal has revived the fame
  Of our lost Perrys and Decaturs ;

When will that day of blood and flame
  Be unremembered by the traitors ?
Our roaring implements of death
  Woke fear and trembling in that city
Where fell Rebellion first drew breath,
  And armed his pirates and banditti.

### XXI.

When " On to Richmond ! " was the cry,
  Talk not of routed thousands flying ;
Dragoons and footmen rushing by,
  Regardless of the dead and dying—
The " Chivalry " far greater speed
  Have shown when meeting with reverses,
Leaving behind them in their need,
  Arms, clothing, wretched scrip and purses.

### XXII.

This government, insulted long,
  By fiends who glory in trangression,
Though patient under grevious wrong
  Now drains the life-blood of Secession.
The sceptred tyrants of the world
  Who thought Columbia's doom was written
Ere sword is sheathed, or banner furled
  By Freedom's gauntlet shall be smitten.

### XXIII.

Old Pharisee of Nations ! pause !
  While covert aid to traitors lending ;
Be wary when a righteous cause,
  Bold, chainless millions are defending.

Deem not stern warning to beware,
　Weak, idle words not worth the heeding;
Your Lion to his island lair
　Twice have we driven maimed and bleeding.

### XXIV.

The leaves of history are black
　With thy iniquities unnumbered,
And darkly ambushed for attack
　In vengeance that too long has slumbered.
In fierce pursuit of power and gold
　The scourge of nations thou has proven:
For thee, like haughty Tyre of old,
　The funeral pall will yet be woven.

### XXV.

We ask no sympathy from thee
　While insurrection frowns defiant,
More strong, grey Robber of the Sea!
　Will tower again this Western Giant.
Hark! to the stormy battle-song
　Of freemen on their march victorious,
And banish hope that fraud and wrong
　Can overthrow this Empire glorious.

## OUR BANNER.

### I.

THE red on our flag is the herald of dawn
While curtains that darken the East are withdrawn

Like thunderbolts launched from the heart of a cloud,
Each stripe lends a gleam to War's sulphury shroud.
Then, while the breath of the tempest shall fan her,
Let *red* have a place on the folds of our banner.

### II.

The white is an emblem of peace to the world
When the black flag of Treason forever is furled—
That stainless in name should the champion be
Who fights with a strong arm for the Land of the Free.
Then, while the breath of the tempest shall fan her,
Let *white* have a place on our glorious banner.

### III.

For clustering stars a rich ground work of blue
Its folds from the dome of the firmament drew,
And the planets of Heaven shall darken with rust
Ere Columbia's ensign is trailed in the dust.
Then, while the breath of the tempest shall fan her,
Let *blue* have a place on the folds of our banner.

### IV.

Up, up for the conflict, ye valiant and true,
And die ere dishonored the " Red, White and Blue ! "
Tear down from its staff the Palmetto and Snake !
While the ranks of Secession grow frightened and break,
To victory ride o'er the dying and dead,
Like the horsemen of Gaul with Murat at their head.

## MARTIAL MUSIC.

### I.

SOUND, sound the Spartan fife ;
　The Persian banners wave,
And, marching to the strife,
　Let music thrill the brave ;
Above the clash of steel,
　The shock of meeting foes,
The charger's clattering heel,
　The ringing twang of bows,
A bolder strain is played,
And Persia flies dismayed.

### II.

Castile is up in arms
　Against the Moor to-day ;
Sword-clang and loud alarms
　Announce the coming fray ;
The atabal is heard,
　Thrown by are light djerreeds,
And, on to conflict spurred,
　Rush, Yemen's milk-white steeds :—
"Il Allah!" loud and high
Their turbaned riders cry.

### III.

Beat time upon the drum—
　A brisker measure play—
Old England's warriors come
　In thunder to the fray.

Their bayonets are bright,
   In blood to redden soon—
Oh ! cheer them to the fight
   With still a bolder tune ;
One shock, and all is o'er—
Crushed foes can form no more.

IV.

Ring, out, wild bugle ! ring
   Thy loudest, clearest note
To horse the troopers spring,
   While plume and pennon float ;
They charge, and fallen lie
   The broken, hollow squares,
While quaver shrill and high,
   Gaul's ancient battle airs ;
Their music valor warms,
And nerves strong hearts and arms.

V.

Blow, plaided piper blow
   Some rousing Highland air,
For the victorious foe
   Back Britain's bravest bear !
The piper louder plays,
   The clans renew the fight,
And while their muskets blaze
   Foes scatter wide in flight ;
For how can Scotland quail
When music cheers the Gael !

VI.

Hark ! ' Hail Columbia ' wakes
　A thrill in free-born breasts ;
The hostile column quakes,
　And shorn are nightly crests ;
Where man encounters man,
　And shot and shell rain fast,
Our banner in the van
　Is flapping on the blast ;
The earth with foemen strown—
A host is overthrown !

## BATTLE CALL.

I.

Up and arm ! Up and arm, for the land is in danger ;
On footmen, and horsemen, and swift rifle ranger ;
Leave shop, office, factory, counters and farms,
While the cry thrills all hearts, one and all fly to arms !
　　Let cowards retreat,
　　While our starred banner-sheet
　　Flaps the gale.

II.

Up and arm ! Up an arm, for the hordes of Secession
Are marching against us, all black with transgression ;

Our thinned ranks of Northmen let freemen recruit,
The soil of the Key-Stone their footsteps pollute :
   Let cowards retreat,
   While our starred banner-sheet
   Flaps the gale.

### III.

Up and arm ! for the soil by our fathers adored !
The best cure for treason are shot, shell and sword :
Then rush like the waves of the sea to the shock,
Let us meet them as met by the surge is the rock.
   Let cowards retreat,
   While our starred banner-sheet
   Flaps the gale.

### IV.

Up and arm for the country of Carroll and Wirt!
Shall freemen the flag of the Union desert ;
Shall Washington fall, while base faction prevails,
And the dagger of Treason our Union assails ?
   Let cowards retreat,
   While our starred banner-sheet
   Flaps the gale.

### V.

Up and arm ! In the thunder and smoke of the strife
My curse on the wretch who would not offer life
In guarding the fabric upreared by our sires,
While blazes on each hill-top the land's beacon fires
   Let cowards retreat,
   While our starred banner-sheet
   Flaps the gale.

VI.

Up and arm ! though the wife of your bosom is dying,
The children you love on their death-beds are lying;
Far better a grave in the soil you defend,
Than dastard, drag out a long life to the end.
　　　Let cowards retreat,
　　　　While our starred banner-sheet
　　　　　Flaps the gale.

---

## ODE.

---

I.

Lo ! stainless as the mountain sleet,
　A chaplet decks Columbia's brow ;
No blot is on her banner-sheet,
　No cloud on her escutcheon now :
A grander, more inspiring lay
Should thrill Earth's mighty heart to-day
Than stirred it when the Red sea coast
Was grim with corpses of a host.

II.

Oh! what a voice of jubilee,
　From liberated millions rose,
When Sherman, marching to the sea,
　With mortal fear alarmed his foes ;

Blood-dripping lash, and clanking chain,
Are banished from our vast domain,
And freedmen cultivate the sod
Where the great captain's war-horse trod.

### III.

Crows, northward winging overhead
   Their way from fields of desperate fight,
Tales of the unreturning dead
   Seem croaking in their heavy flight :—
Long absent they are flocking back
To olden haunts in funeral black,
And may their beaks in precious gore
Of brethren steeped be nevermore.

### IV.

Peace to the fallen ! hostile thought,
   And vengeful vow should be supprest
Since the great conflict has been fought,
   And Union's cause with triumph blest.
Bones of our perished warriors lie,
Land of the South ! beneath thy sky,
And dust of northern hearts must be,
" Till crack of doom," a part of thee.

### V.

And where war rolled his purple waves
   Through thy broad realm the generous West
Won partnership with thee in graves
   Where martyrs of the struggle rest.
Friends now, but late thy foes, we feel
That thou wert worthy of our steel,
And that thy sons, in league with ours,
Could tame a bad world's banded powers.

### VI.

Victorious, we scorn to tear
   One leaf, in view of Stonewall's tomb
From laurel thine the right to wear,
   One feather from thy battle plume:
Ere slavery died unwept, unsung,
A plague-spot to thy beauty clung:
New-trimmed thine alter-flame to-day
Emits a purer, holier ray.

### VII.

Between stern North and fiery South,
   Although a thousand hopes are wrecked,
Acquaintance at the cannon's mouth
   Begot a mutual respect.
The brave resentment never know
When overthrown a gallant foe,
Baptised by fire and leaden rain,
Who measured strength with them in vain.

### VIII.

No longer like red levin glows
   Bellona's torch from shore to shore ;
With autumn leaves and wintry snows
   Its embers have been covered o'er ;
And richer for the bloody toil
Of foemen is the quickened soil,
And growing on heroic graves,
With ranker growth the harvest waves.

### IX.

The fiery passions of the strife
   Thus in the hearts of men will die,

And flowers of love and nobler life
   Spring up where cold their ashes lie :—
Again the myrtle loves to twine
Its blossoms round the northern pine,
And healing winds are breathing balm
Upon the wounded southern palm.

## SHENANDOAH VALLEY.

### I.

Lo! Shenandoah from its source,
And, northward, where it runs its course,
   Flows with a mournful murmur, on ;
Town-spires have vanished, one by one,
They flash not in the setting sun,
   Nor catch the glow of dawn.

### II

The reddened hoof of Battle, shod
With thunder, through thy vale hath trod
   So often that nor song of bird,
Nor pastoral music as of yore
   Is near thy mournful current heard
Imbued with fratricidal gore :
Hearths of once happy homes are cold,
The shepherd finds no flock to fold ;
Away marauding bands have spurred
Driving the last steer of thé herd,

And nought betokens even life
Where raged the roar and rush of strife,
Save, howling for the hand that fed,
　　The watch-dog with his famished form,
Or wanderer, in affluence bred,
Without a place to lay his head,
　　Or house him from the storm.

### III.

The smithy lies in ruin low,
The bellows hath forgot to blow;
Unstirred by bell-stroke in the air
When Sabbath brings a call to prayer;
Hushed is the clatter of the mill—
The hum of Industry is still;
A pall is o'er the hamlet thrown,
Gray ashes mark its site alone;
And grim with half-uncovered graves,
Too thick to number like thy waves,
　　Are fields of mortal conflict seen
The wolf alluring from his lair
To hold, with flocking ravens, there
　　A carnival obscene.

### IV.

Wyoming! valley, famed in song,
Where right waged war with lawless wrong,
Thou wert a region of delight,
When o'er thy memorable fight,
Compared with Shenandoah's vale
Where every land-mark tells a tale
　　Of ruin, wo and blight.

Rich carpets, gilded picture-frames,
   Heir-looms that told of "Long Ago,"
Gay Cavaliers, and courtly dames
Were flung, *rich fuel*, to the flames.
   While bivouacked the foe.

---

## TOURNAMENT OF DEATH;

### OR,

### READ'S LAST RIDE.

---

### I.

Rich in proud memories is the pass
Where perished of old Leonidas,
His precious blood libation free
Poured out at the shrine of liberty :
But this mighty world of the West can boast
As great a name in freedom's host,
To grandly peal in a nation's shout,
When our banner of stars is flaming out,
Inspiring men in the desperate fight
To conquer, or die for God and the Right.
    Then crown with laurel, Read !
    With deathless laurel, Read !
    For never rode in glory's van
    A braver, or a better man,
      Upon his battle steed.

## II.

The spurring courier tidings brought
That junction Lee with Johnston sought,
Determined, although great his loss,
The Appomattox bridge to cross,
And changing base the war prolong
With a force an hundred thousand strong,
Read hurried, with a weak array,
To bring the southern chief to bay,
Though suffering from wounds unhealed
Received on many a desperate field.
    Then crown with laurel, Read !
    With deathless laurel, Read !
    For never rode in glory's van
    A braver, or a better man,
      Upon his battle steed.

## III.

When reached his post of peril dire
He shouted, while his eye flashed fire,
" We must hold this bridge, my lads ! or die—
If they pass it must be where our corpses lie."
With fearful odds the foe rushed on,
Drums beat the charge, and blades were drawn,
But the *blue* jackets charged the *grey*,
And the head of their column was swept away.
    Then crown with laurel, Read !
    With deathless laurel, Read !
    For never rode in glory's van
    A braver, or a better man,
      Upon his battle steed.

### IV.

Again, and again were driven back
The Rebel ranks in their fierce attack ;
Where man met man, and steed met steed
Charged, under spur, the gallant Read :
Never Murat of the snow-white plume,
Whose shout was an army's knell of doom,
Fought on with more of skill and might
In the red maelstrom of the fight,
And cheered by foes was this warrior true
Leading to death his devoted few.
  Then crown with laurel, Read !
  With deathless laurel, Read !
  For never rode in glory's van
  A braver, or a better man,
   Upon his battle steed.

### V.

Though bleeding fast, with sword in hand,
While melted away his Spartan band,
Read marked a general of the foe
Tower in their van for the final blow,
But he shouted, with a flashing eye,
" We must hold the bridge, my lads, or die !"—
Then met in the shock of fearful fight,
The rebel chief, like a belted knight,
While dead from their steeds that bore them well
*Both*, in that stern encounter, fell.
  Then crown with laurel, Read !
  With deathless laurel, Read !
  For never rode in glory's van
  A braver, or a better man,
   Upon his battle steed.

### VI.

Thus the back-bone of treason broke,
For Lee received his mortal stroke
When Read in manhood's glorious morn,
Made battle with his "hope forlorn,"
While crimson from their wounds outwelled,
And Appomattox Bridge was held.
On fame's unmoulding column traced,
High will this feat of arms be placed,
And all who perished on that day
In the nation's heart be enshrined. for aye.
    Then crown with laurel, Read !
    With deathless laurel, Read !
    For never rode in glory's van
    A braver, or a better man,
      Upon his battle steed.

## SONG.

### I.

JEFF's Kingdom of Cotton with infamy rotten
  Was doomed to succumb to our glorious flag ;
The brave rallied under the stars while in thunder
  Was torn into shreds his piratical rag,
The stream. from its fountain, on Look Out's proud
    mountain,
  Hath drank flowing down a libation of blood ;
The doom of transgression has smitten secession
  Where dark Chattanooga rolls onward his flood.

II.

Shout loud, ho, hosannah ! the stripes o'er Savannah,
  Red symbols of doom to proud tyranny wave,
Stern Justice hath risen, and lo ! from his prison
  Bursts Freedom announcing redress to the slave.
False South ! heed the sermon that practical Sherman,
  From mouths of his cannon propounded to you ;
His legions are chaunting—"weighed well, and
    found wanting."
  Are wretches who trod on the "Red, White and
    Blue."

III.

Proud Charleston is humbled. for Sumter hath crum-
    bled,
  To ruin her storm-beaten battlements hurled ;
That eloquent preacher of liberty, Beecher,
  Her funeral oration pronounced to the world.
Our famished and dying in dungeons were lying
  Where batteries frowned on the banks of the James ;
No longer they languish—forgotten their anguish
  In Sheridan's march, and the roaring of flames.

IV.

Death only brings terror to black guilt and error,
  His skull-bones affright not the just and the true ;
What shroud for the martyr who loves Freedom's
    charter
    More prized than the glorious "Red, White and
      Blue ?"
Our eagle his pinion once more, Old Dominion !
  Flaps o'er you while Earth hears his conquering cry ;
The bright bow of promise, so long absent from us,
  Again arches over Columbia's sky.

## OUR LOYAL DEAD.

### I.

OUR martyred dead, our martyred dead !
  The land is billowed with their graves ;
Sods were uptorn to make their bed
  While rolled the battle's purple waves :
Few, near their shrouded fathers rest,
With funeral flowers their couches drest.

### II.

Ah ! thousands worn, and famine-pale
  Died captives of the cruel foe,
No mourner save the blast to wail
  Where famished men were lying low ;
While the hill-tops catch morning's flame
Their native North will guard their fame.

### III.

Rust will consume the blades they drew,
  Moths eat the banner that the bore,
But deeds of men to Freedom true
  In generous hearts live evermore ;
Time drops his scythe, and Death flings by
His dart, when heroes nobly die.

### IV.

Their mission ends not when the goal
  Of life through blood and toil they gain,
Although the muffled bells we toll
  While slow move hearse and funeral train ;
Crushed cages of the soul we bear,
But where the spirit ?—tell me where ?

### V.

Inspiring hearts whose pulses keep
   Time to the battle-march of truth,
Waking the bondsman from his sleep,
   And giving age a second youth :
Though echoless their footsteps fall
I see their shadows on the wall.

### VI.

Along my nerves their whispers low
   Awaken an electric thrill ;
They come to share our joy and woe,
   Are living, loving, breathing still ;
By man's dim, clouded gaze unseen
The dead, to-night, with us convene.

### VII.

Ye mourners ! throw your weeds away, ·
   Let no wild requiem be sung ;
The voices of the slain all day
   Have in mine ear like harp-notes rung :
We number them with bright things fled,
But *they* exist whom *we* call dead.

### VIII.

Spectators, listeners ! they have heard
   The words that from my tongue have rolled,
And, when my heart grew faint, have stirred
   My bosom with the fires of old :
Although unseen by mortal sight
The dead move, in our midst, to-night.

### IX

Assure them, ere they cross again
   The cold, dark stream that knows no tide,
Whose waves the realm where seraphs reign
   From this dark land of storm divide,
A generous band will pay the debt
Of gratitude we owe them yet.

### X.

Up with the monumental tower,
   Or rear the cenotaph on high,
In honor of our dead—the flower
   Of Livingston's proud chivalry:
Kind ladies! men of generous mould,
Part with your jewels, rings and gold!

### XI.

Crown with a shaft of marble pale,
   Or granite gray, yon upland swell
That overlooks a lovelier vale
   Than Arno's, of which poets tell,
In honor of the brave who died
That Union's ark the wave might ride.

### XII.

While by our household fires we sit
   Recall the lads who dared to die
When, crimson to each bridle-bit,
   The steeds of havoc thundered by—
Died that this league of States might be
Soldered with blood eternally.

### XIII.

When we forget our loyal dead
  Who nobly fell for hearth and shrine,
Black be the pall o'er nature spread,
  Our valley red with blood like wine :
Then let their funeral shaft uptower
A rallying place in danger's hour.

---

## DECORATION DAY.

### I.

COMETH from bright, Elysian fields,
Air that such balmy odor yields,
Or is it sweetened by the breath
Of Flora at the gates of death ?
Immortelles, reaped on holy ground,
Wreath the Pale Mower's scythe around,
While flits the phantom of a smile
His ashen visage o'er the while.

### II.

Marble forget-me-nots of art
Lone grandeur to the tomb impart
Linked, towering precious dust above
To pride, not sentiments of love,
'Till wreaths fair hands delight to form,
Their monumental coldness warm,
Tears in each cup, and chalice bright
Dropped by the star eyed mourner, Night.

### III.

The fancy of the gifted Greek
Through language of the flowers would speak ;
Mute pathos of each withering leaf
Gave to bruised hearts a blest relief
When childhood died, or early lost
On beauty fell destroying frost :—
Thus Pericles of sternest mould
Wept, crowning Paralus of old.

### IV.

Oh ! to the nation's heart how dear
Dust of the martyrs buried here ;
Long in this Greenwood of the soul
For them may voices call the roll !
To sepulchres in which they lie,
With frozen pulse and curtained eye,
May future generations pay
The reverent care we show to-day.

### V.

Give to the pansy, streaked with jet,
Place in a funeral coronet
Beside the lily of the vale
To grace tall shaft, or headstone pale.
Forget not, ye that mourn, between
Frail buds to weave the evergreen,
Sign that the faithful dead will be
Kept ever green in memory.

### VI.

From Holy Writ we learn, alas !
" Man's glory as the flower of grass "

Blooms for a bright, and fleeting day
Then fades, and vanisheth away.
Meet, therefore, for these grassy beds,
Where pillowed lie heroic heads,
Are garlands, wet with tearful showers,
Culled from the sisterhood of flowers.

### VII.

Tri-colored blossoms thickly spread
Over each warrior's narrow bed, |
In tint and shade conforming well
With the dear flag for which they fell.
Bring roses of auroral glow,
Lilies that shame the mountain snow,
And to complete the colors three,
Bring blue bells from the Genesee.

### VIII.

The " Flower of Love lies bleeding" well
With mute significance will tell
How mothers of the martyred brave
Were brought in sorrow to the grave ;
How wife, and broken-hearted maid
Still mourn for valor lowly laid,
And widowhood of sable veil,
Sobs out wild dirge-notes to the gale.

### IX.

In spirit on this hallowed day,
I visit hillocks far away,
And over them I long to fling
Bright, floral treasures of the Spring.

There son and brother moulder on,
While Love grows pale and woe-begone'
To think, on mounds of their repose,
Not one poor native wild-flower grows.

### X.

Fain would I grace blood-moistened earth
With tributes from their place of birth;
The dandelion's brooch of gold
Pluck from the tartan of the wold,
Or common flowers that smile at morn,
Near the lost homes where they were born,
To whisper on each lorn, drear spot,
" One faithful heart forgets ye not ! "

### XI

Endeared is Albion's chalky strand
By sports of merry Motherland
When dancing feet of nymphs kept time
Round May-poles, to soft music's chime ;
And on the daisied village green
Crowned was a young and blushing queen,—
But doubly dear henceforth is May
Hallowed by " Decoration Day."

### XII.

Oh! is it not a thought sublime
That at this blest, appointed time,
From dark Atlantic's coast-line grand
To far Pacific's golden strand,—
From orient hills in purple drest
To prairies of the mighty West ;
From Northland to Floridian· bowers,
Heroic graves are strewn with flowers.

### XIII.

With leaves that "sad embroidery" wear
From field and grove cull wildlings rare
To symbolize our speechless woe
For rank and file, laid early low,
That nevermore one bondsman's chain
Might clank on Freedom's broad domain,
And, blood-cemented, to the skies
Our temple, block by block, might rise.

### XIV.

The "Mountain Daisy," by the plow
Of Burns upturned, is blooming now,
More fortunate than sister flowers,
It fades not with the fleeting hours;
And honored well will be the bard,
Thrice blest, no longer evil-starred,
If, song embalmed, to perish never,
These funeral wreaths bloom on forever.

# BITTER MEMORIES.

# MY STUDY.

### I.

I am not lonely in my quiet room,
  Though nought of mortal shape is near me now,
While wanes my taper in the deepening gloom,
  And drops af studious toil are on my brow ;
Against my window chafes the leafless bough,
  Drear sign that birds and flowers no more delight
And, sweeter than young Love's first, whispered vow
  Æolian voices quaver while I write,
As if they sung the dirge of melancholy night.

### II.

On the arched gateway, near my office door,
  With head erect a carven, couchant hound
Seems shivering in the blast of winter hoar,
  And watching for his master, homeward bound ;—
Flecked by the starlight is the frozen ground      •
  As if the dead were parting with their shrouds ;
The drifting snow gives out a muffled sound,
  Like din remote of mighty, mustering crowds,
While through the fields of Heaven float stormy, air
    borne clouds.

### III.

Dimly illumined is the pictured wall
  Where flitting shadows hurry to and fro ;

On painted forms, and scenes my glances fall,
  While back returns a dream of Long Ago ;
I see loved streams, with music in their flow,
  Within whose waves in youth I cast the line,
And woods where, hunting, spared were fawn and doe
  Through love for babe and wife, no longer mine,
Translated to a land where reigneth Love Divine.


### IV.

Quaint books are on the shelves, well thumbed and
    old,
  Chaucer our morning star—and Spencer, king
Of a weird realm, with purple draped and gold,
  Sitting enthroned in an enchanted ring ;
Immortals, breathing an eternal spring,
  "Rare Ben," "Sweet Will," and others, world-
    renowned,
Back the grand age of Albion's Virgin bring ;
  Writers that walked, by Cam and Isis, gowned,
And bards, neglected now, of yore with laurel crowned.


### V.

The master-spirits of the Solemn Past
  Still in their works are living, breathing here,
But how can one whose soul is overcast
  Con o'er the lettered tomes of bard and seer ?
From far-off shores a mystic voice I hear
  That calls on me to finish tasks begun,
With the stern warning—"lo ! the goal is near !
  Soon will thy darkened thread of life be spun,
And chaplet for thy brow, when marble-cold, be won."

## A LAMENT—WRITTEN AT SEA.

### I.

With an angry sea before us,
While dark, gray clouds float o'er us
    We're drifting to and fro;
The spicy gales have left us,
A wintry chill bereft us
    Of summer's tropic glow.

### II.

With head winds bravely battling,
Our ship with cordage rattling
    Rides on the emerald crest;
The wildest roar of ocean
Can wake no dread emotion
    In my despairing breast.

### III.

Man, when the *worst* he knoweth,
Although the whirlwind bloweth,
    Is self-possessed and calm;
For when the heart is breaking,
Forever, ever aching,
    Where is the healing balm?

### IV.

I think of one who sleepeth,
While many a mourner weepeth,
    Untimely lost and drowned;
In dreams, tossed on the billow,
He sits near my rude pillow
    With angel beauty crowned.

5

### V.

I know his spirit hovering
Is near when night is covering
   The waters with her pall;
And for sweet Willie grieving
I start from sleep believing
   I hear once more his call.

### VI.

Oh ! what a wild, deep yearning
I feel for the returning
   Of my brave, gifted boy;
And yew and cypress throwing
A funeral gloom, are growing
   Upon the grave of joy.

### VII.

Hark·! in mine ear is ringing
A voice more sweet than singing:
   "I've seen the radiant shore
Where Death can triumph never,
And youth blooms on forever—
   Dear Father! mourn no more."

---

## EPECEDIUM.

### I.

THE sumach, colored like a dying ember,
  Proclaims the race of fiery Summer o'er;
Resigning crown and throne to mild September,
    She reigns no more.

II.

Not only radiant Summer hath departed,
  But a dear friend has left this darkened clime ;
One nobly gifted, pure and gentle-hearted
    Is done with time.

III.

Again will summer come back with the swallow,
  Bearing a rose-wreathed sceptre in her hand,
And airy beings in her train will follow
    From Fairy-Land ;

IV

Again will Earth, arrayed in rich apparel,
  The bloom and freshness of its youth renew,
And skies that listen to the lark's wild carol,
    Be robed in blue.

V.

But who come back to still the restless yearning
  In aching bosoms, from Death's chill domain ?
With prayers and tears we wait for their returning,
    In vain, in vain !

VI.

Faster and faster from his ghostly quiver,
  By the Pale Archer deadly shafts are drawn ;
With every breath, across the still, black river,
    Another's gone.

VII.

" We are such stuff as dreams are made of," singeth
  With thrilling power earth's grandly gifted son ;
And ere the seed we plant in toil upspringeth,
    Our work is done.

### VIII.

How weak are mortals in their best condition !
How frail the tenure of an earthly trust !
On every wind we hear the stern monition
Of "dust to dust ! "

### IX.

Ye childless parents of the dead ! oft fated
Are the heart's idols first to pass away
From this dark sphere—we cherish hope, translated
To endless day.

### X.

The canker feeds upon the sweetest roses,
And shafts spare not the bird of brightest plume ;
On Beauty's brow the pale seal oft reposes
Of early doom.

### XI.

What consolation can the mourner borrow
From an affliction like the one ye bear ?
What lenitive can cure the pangs of sorrow
Your hearts that tear?

### XII.

The blissful thought that he hath left behind him
A stainless name—a record without blot—
And well fulfilled the tasks that were assigned him,
And faltered not.

### XIII.

The blissful thought that noble emulation
Fired his brave, generous spirit to the last ;
His aim, a proud position in the nation
When youth was past.

### XIV.

The blissful thought that war and wild commotion
  Vex not the quiet realm that claims your son ;
While ye are tossed upon a troubled ocean,
      His port is won.

### XV.

If skill were mine the wondrous harp to waken
  That sang of " Lycidas without a peer,"
A dirge more worthy friend so early taken
      The world should hear.

### XVI.

But all a bard whose soul is crushed and broken
  Can give, by way of tribute, I bestow,
Though nothing more than sighings that betoken
      His utter wo.

### XVII.

Better to perish in the happy morning,
  Than travel through the day with fainting form,
Night coming on, with thunder-mutter warning,
      In darkness—storm ;

### XVIII.

Perish before the soul is disenchanted,
  And turns with loathing from the things of time,
To find the world it clung to demon-haunted,
      And foul with crime.

## MY OLD COMRADE.

### I.

KEEN, darting wit that wounded not the heart
At which was aimed his brightly polished dart ;
Quaint humor that gave colloquy a zest,
While laughter followed every harmless jest ;
A soul to meanness that could not descend,
Were traits that marked my dear departed friend.
He was not for the fashion of these times,
And praised the ring of Father Chaucer's rhymes ;
Better he loved weird Spencer to peruse
Than glittering couplets of the modern muse,
And with advancing years prized more and more
The crystal well-head of Shaksperean lore.

### II.

He held in veneration, deepest awe,
Black-lettered tomes of Anglo-Saxon law,
And Bracton, Coke, to him were dearer names
Than Kent and Story, although great their claims.
Sitting as judge, learnèd counsellors in vain
Would use their skill to cloud his active brain ;
He brushed their webs of sophistry aside
With common sense—a sure, unerring guide—
Bringing to mind the stern, judicial sway
Of men who wore the robe in Blackstone's day.

### III.

Field sports he loved : from rise till set of sun
Oft would he range the woods with dog and gun,
Rest from the heat of noon at some wild spring,
And the old songs of Allan Ramsey sing,

Or wake the landscape from its slumber mute
With silvery echoes of his well-played flute;
He loved old Walton's art, and threw the fly
With a firm hand, and true unerring eye;
And while regaling on some grassy bank,
His comrade cheered with merry quip and crank.

### IV.

Ah! when the star of such a one has set
How deeply filled the soul is with regret;
Earth is too poor in men of mould like him
To lose them in the land of shadows dim—
To hear pale Grief above their ashes pour
Groans answered by that grim word "nevermore!"

## WAYSIDE RHYMES.

### I.

SICK of the dust and din of trade,
Weary of noise by Mammon made,
And intercourse with living lies,
Poor, gilded cheats in mortal guise,
And Fashion's gaudy butterflies
I left for Nature's greenwood halls
The gloom of close, confining walls,
And sought cool arbors, dim and still,
That lend enchantment to Glenrill,
And where Oatka's waters roll
Held audience with my own sad soul.

### 11.

Oh ! what a luxury to lie
  On the mossed forest floor alone,
  And when aside the boughs are blown,
Catch glimpses of the deep, blue sky !
  Thus in an idlesse mood I lay
  While closed the long, midsummer day ;
Each nodding wild flower, wind-swept leaf
Sang a low lullaby to grief ;
  Birds warbled from their pulsing throats
  Condoling, sympathizing notes,
Until I thought, opprest and ill,
That Nature's offspring loved me still,
  And knew their worshipper—though gone
  The glory of his golden dawn :
The power to wake, from day to day,
The sounding legend and the lay :
  The gifted vision to descry
  Shapes rarely seen by mortal eye.

### III.

Sleep, like a blessing, on me fell
  While rustled over me the trees,
And music of the pastoral bell
  Was wafted by me on the breeze.
Although my visual orbs were sealed
  I saw with open, spirit eyes,
From catacomb, and battle field,
  Sites of lost marts, sepulchral caves,
  Earth's nameless, unrecorded graves,
Gray bards and warriors rise.
Trenched were their brows with scars of conflict fought
On storied plains, and in the realm of thought ;

Ah! they could look behind this outward veil
  And read the firm, fixed purpose of my soul
O'er syrens of temptation to prevail,
  And exercise a lofty self-control.
They knew the crosses I had borne,
  The paths of fearful peril I had trod,
  At times forlorn, forsaken as of God,
And pitying gazed upon my heart-strings torn.

IV.

  Rang, like a clarion, loud and clear
  From august lips these words of cheer :
    " Be patient under suffering, and your load
  Bear, like the Saviour, on a thorny road ;
    Temptation made us strong ;
The noblest spirits must be crucified,
By the fierce furnace of affliction tried
Ere clothed with might to conquer hideous Wrong.
    Some of our number died
Outstretched upon the rack of torture dire,
And others perished at the stake by fire ;
The agony is o'er, the guerdon won,
Angelic lips have warbled out well done ! ' '

V.

Oh ! palm-crowned spirits of the mighty Dead,
These words brought healing to a heart that bled ;
    Ye knew my struggle to refrain
From the charmed cup of Circe drugged with bane ;
My stern adherence to a solemn vow
  When Pleasure, dazzling sorceress, tried her spell
And strove in vain to write upon my brow
    The hieroglyph of Hell ;

They knew that Slander, wearing truth's fair cloak
  In ear of one more dear than life or light,
  The guiding star of my tempestuous night,
Had blistering words of foulest falsehood spoke.

## THE MOTHER'S APPEAL.

### I.

"Bring back my dead!"
Thus cried the mother of a boy
  Who fell in battle slain;
Source of her greatest hope and joy
  For whom she wails in vain.

### II.

"Bring back my dead!"
Beneath our starry banner's fold
  He yielded up his life—
Alas! for such a heart grown cold
  In this infernal strife.

### III.

"Bring back my dead!"
He was an infant in my lap,
  I nursed him on my breast;
Although he wore no shoulder strap
  He battled with the best.

IV.

" Bring back my dead ! "
My lips have touched the bitter cup
   Of sorrow and despair;
His precious life is offered up,
   The loss I cannot bear.

V.

" Bring back my dead ! "
His sister has a lonely grave,
   No buried brother nigh;
Give my young warrior a grave
   Beneath his native sky.

VI.

" Bring back my dead ! "
The Rappahannock rolls its flood
   Where comrades dug his grave,
And in his blanket, soaked with blood,
   He sleeps—bring back my Brave !

VII.

" Bring back my dead ! "
Far dearer are the cold remains
   Than any living one;
On thy bright memory are no stains
   Of guilt, my darling son !

VIII.

" Bring back my dead ! "
The leaves of autumn, far away,
   Fall on the burial-mound ;
Secession's curse is on the clay,
   It is unholy ground.

### IX.

"Bring back my dead!"
Victorious over death and night
  The cannon rung his knell;
A martyr in the cause of right
  My beardless hero fell.

### X.

"Bring back my dead!"
Uncoffined on the field he sleeps,
  My Beautiful and Brave,
And watch Columbia's Genius keeps
  Beside his unmarked grave.

### XI.

"Bring back my dead!"
In soil by foul Rebellion cursed
  He cannot slumber well;
Here in this valley was he nursed,
  Here toll his funeral bell.

### XII.

"Bring back my dead!"
I see him in my nightly dreams,
  His brow is fresh and fair;
Endowed with health and hope he seems,
  No mark of carnage there.

### XIII.

"Bring back my dead!"
Far dearer are his cold remains
  Than any living one;
On his bright memory are no stains,
  Bring back, bring back my son!

## LINES WRITTEN IN DEJECTION NEAR "WIL-
## LOW MOUNT," AVON, N. Y.

### I.

WHY from my aching heart is banished gladness,
  Why seems the ghost of desolation near,
Why is my mood one of prevailing sadness?
    Thou art not here.

### II.

Why in the midnight deep am I awaking
  While the wan ghosts of memory appear,
And farewell mourning Love of Hope seems taking?
    Thou art not here.

### III.

Why in my bosom thrill the chords of sorrow,
  While mournful music falls upon the ear,
Why from my book and pen no comfort borrow?
    Thou art not here.

### IV.

I toil alone heart-broken, sick, unaided,
  While Winter's bitter blast chants dirges drear;
With funeral black both earth and sky are shaded:
    Thou art not here.

### V.

When will I hear again that voice far sweeter
  Than flute-notes heard on moon-lit waters clear?
I cannot waken to melodious metre:
    Thou art not here!

### VI.

Star of my being! will thy lustre never
   To one adoring send a beam of cheer,
Or have we parted, darling one! forever?
    Would thou wert here!

### VII.

Would I had wings to conquer cruel distance
   That I might fly thy seraph voice to hear!
Thou art the light and life of my existence—
    Would thou wert here!

### VIII.

I feel like one who sees, all shrouded lying,
   The last who loved him on the dismal bier,
And murmurs words she faltered out while dying—
    Thou art not here.

### IX.

There is a kingdom, bright beyond expression,
   That cannot be portrayed by bard or seer;
Thither our lost ones march in pale procession,
    The dead, the dear.

### X.

Not dead, but to a better land translated
   Where never wailing cry woke mystic fear,
And I, with life's poor, fleeting pleasure sated,
    Long for that sphere.

### XI.

Oh! naught could make me pause, ere crossed death's
    waters,
   Chill as the blast with icebergs floating near,
Save one, the purest, fairest of Eve's daughter's,
    Who is not here.

### XII.

My bark long tossed upon the breakers foaming
  To a calm port of Peace I fain would steer,
And build a nuptial bower, no longer roaming,
    For one not here.

### XIII.

Vain are such dreams, and worse than vain complain
    ing:
  Earth boasts no cure for agony like mine,
The lees alone are in my cup remaining
    Gone, gone, Life's wine.

---

## HERETOFORE.

" From all its kind this wasted heart,
This moody mind now drifts apart;
It longs to find the tideless shore
Where rests the wreck of Heretofore."—

MOTHERWELL.

### I.

Fresh are the roses of to-day
  With hues that match the sunset's glow,
But sweeter, dearer far than they
  Are flowers that withered long ago ;
Young flowers that graced a radiant shore
Washed by the waves of Heretofore.

### II.

Take back this tome with gilded leaves,
　　The work of one by woe untaught ;
The soul of constancy that grieves
　　Within can find no room for thought :
I love alone to ponder o'er
The blotted scroll of Heretofore.

### III.

Names written on that record dim,
　　And stained with unavailing tears,
While airy visions round me swim,
　　Bring back the joys of other years ;
And beams, outshining noontide, pour
Through the torn clouds of Heretofore.

### IV.

Discordant to my mood of mind
　　Is music of the present hour,
For only in the past I find
　　A voice that hath a spell of power ;
A voice that wakes to life once more
The buried forms of Heretofore.

### V.

I love the home, so glad of old,
　　Though damp and mouldy now its walls,
And converse sweet with phantoms hold
　　That glide at midnight through its halls,
For they are wanderers from the shore
Of thy dim realm, oh, Heretofore !

### VI.

Kind looks, as slowly they depart,
   On me the wan procession cast,
For well they know that one poor heart
   Keeps green remembrance of the past—
A heart that trembles to its core,
When sung the songs of Heretofore.

### VII.

I love old oaks that feebly wave,
   And weeds that hide a ruined hearth ;
Pale moss upon a sunken grave,
   And every crumbling wreck of earth,
For they are teachers of a lore
That lends a charm to Heretofore.

---

## NEW YEAR MUSINGS.

### I.

How swiftly pass, on cloudy wing, the years,
With all their joys and woes, their hopes and fears,
Bound to a dark, dead sea that knows no sail,
Nor billow foam-flecked by the ruffling gale ;
The vast receptacle of empires dead,
Heroic shapes, and dreams of glory fled,
Within whose peaceful depths of silence lie
All that of mortal memory can die.

### II.

Come back, ye vanished hours ! and bring again
Forms of the loved and lost, bewailed in vain ;
Bring me lost May-time, with its rosy wreath,
And change to Fairy-land life's " blasted heath ! "
Bring me the romance that so warmed of old,
Giving to common clay the gleam of gold.
Once more, once more, ye vanished hours, return !
For the sweet dreams of innocence I yearn.
Oh ! let me feel the calm that once I felt
When, at my mother's knee, in prayer I knelt,
And, starred with hope, my fair, unclouded brow
Told no sad tale of lines that seam it now ;
When my brave brother, who untimely died,
Stood in his rosy beauty by my side ;
Forget, a few brief moments, that my life
Must pass away in storm and doubtful strife—
That nought is certain underneath the skies
Save useless tears, and tombs, and broken ties :
And feel those throbbings of tumultuous joy
That swelled my bosom when a shouting boy ;
The burning glow that flushed my cheek to read
Of martyr, patriot and chivalric deed,
And catch one ray of the strange light that made
Earth in Elysian loveliness arrayed.

### III.

I call—but no responsive echo wakes ;
Through the black cloud no beam of beauty breaks ;
Gone are emotions that my soul up-bore,
Tossed on the sea, or standing on the shore :

The stern, relentless past will not restore
One grain of vanished time, that man awhile
May warm his frozen veins in childhood's smile.
Youth ! a frail, tender violet of the Spring,
Lies in his misty tomb, a withered thing ;
And though our bosoms ache, our tear-drops flow,
We cannot wrest one flower from Long-Ago.

# CYPRESS LEAVES.

## THE TRANCE.

### I.

Mourners were mutely gathered round a bier,
On which reposed the coffin of a child.
With hurried step and wildly-flowing hair
The mother came, and when the lid was raised,
Thus gave expression to her frantic woe :—

### II.

" Make way ! unfeeling crowd !
Heart-broken let me gaze upon my dead
Before ye bear him to his narrow bed.
    Fold back the shroud !
The wind shall kiss his pallid cheek once more
Its touch, perchance, the life-flush may restore.

### III.

" Though pale that face,
The wonted smile of joy it yet retains—
Too much of beauty for the grave remains
    To hide in its embrace.
He sleeps as calmly in that box enclosed
As if within his cradle he reposed.

### IV.

" Look on the sleepers now !
His silken curls are by the soft wind fanned,
A rose-bud blushes in his little hand,
    Torn from the parent bough.
Though death hath made my bud of promise cold
Where angels dwell the leaves may yet unfold,

### v.

" Spreading thy raven wing,
Why blast the lovely long before their prime,
Ere they have felt the wasting touch of time,
　　Pale, shadowy king ?
Why rob the casket of its precious gem,
And pluck the young flower from its tender stem ?

### vi.

" Blight with thy breath
The aged pilgrim in this vale of tears,
Whose form is bending with the weight of years,
　　Insatiate tyrant, Death !
Snatch not the infant from its mother's breast,
Lifeless and cold beneath the sod to rest.

### viii.

" Lo ! I am childless left !
The staff on which I hoped to lean is gone ;
Through life alone I now shall journey on,
　　Of all I loved bereft.
One spirit more hath left the earth to dwell
With kindred souls.　My stricken flower farewell ! "

### ix.

" Mother ! " he faintly cries.
Perchance it was a vagary of the brain—
It cannot be !—those pale lips move again,
　　And open are his eyes !
With the life-flush his cheek is growing red—
" My cup of joy is full—he is not dead ! "

# TRIBUTE

TO THE MEMORY OF THE LATE REV. JACOB BRODHEAD, D. D

———

### I.

Why are the gray-haired fathers of the Church
Convened within these consecrated walls ?
Why altar-piece and pulpit hung with black,
While peals a requiem on the summer air,
And heads, in deep solemnity, are bowed ?
A guiding light is quenched, that long hath thrown
Its steady radiance on life's troubled sea,
Like the tall watch-fire, on some beetling cliff,
Hailed by benighted seamen o'er the waves.
A loved and venerated form will walk
On mercy's errand in our midst no more ;
His mission is accomplished, and the tomb
Opens its portals for the honored dead.

### II.

Better than riches, or the robes of pride,
Are the bright graces of the pure in heart.
The clay-walls of the prison crumble down—
Earth to her breast receives the cast-off robe—
But acts of goodness, oft in secret done,
Unasked-for visitations to the dens
Where mute Remorse lies housed with pleading Woe
Embalm their memory forever more ;
And Heavenly harp-strings, by angelic hands,
Are grandly swept when their enfranchised souls
Soar upward, lark-like, to the Better Land.
6

### III.

True to his sacred office labored on
Our venerated father to the last,
And when the summons that we all must hear,
Was whispered by Death's Angel, with a smile
He heard the tidings, and his last good-bye
Had in it more of welcome than farewell.
How rich the legacy he left ! how poor
Are the mere gauds of fortune, or the shouts
That herald stern Ambition on his way,
While martial music surges on the wind,
And banner-staffs untwine their golden folds—
Compared with greeting looks and heart-warm smiles,
The free spontaneous offerings of love,
When all who knew him saw his face benign !

### IV.

The loved who leave us are not always lost;
They die not like the perishable leaves,
Or summer roses of so brief a date ;
And one like him, who influenced for good,
In public and in private life, the world,
Lives on in grateful hearts where he has sown
The precious seeds of charity and love,
When the dumb earth to her maternal arms
Takes back the loan of poor dissolving clay.

### V.

A soldier of the Church, he nobly fought
The fight of faith, and bore the blessed cross,
Without a stain upon his sacred robe,
Until his long, bright pilgrimage is o'er.

Not without record sleeps he in the grave :
The blessings that he showered upon his flock,
His pure example and advice and alms,
With Christ-like meekness on the poor bestowed,
And the pale crowd of suppliants that choke
The ways of this sad world, are written down
And registered in Heaven.

VI.

Mourn not for him !
Ripe for the harvest he has passed away,
And still the light of his departure calm
Lingers round places that have known him long,
Like the illumined track of vanished day.

## DALE CEMETERY, AT SING-SING.

I.

I love thy hallowed limits, Place of Graves !
    I love the quiet of thy hills and dells,
Where the lone dash of Hudson's wintry waves,
    Softened by distance, like a dirge-note swells :
Those who can look on scenes so fair, unmoved,
Have never Nature loved.

## II.

When o'er the war of life, who would not rest
    From toil and trouble in a place so sweet,—
Rounded the funeral mound above his breast,
    Far from the din of throngs and trampling feet?
Here Grief throws by her sables, and puts on
A golden smile like dawn.

## III.

Those who were dear to me in other days    '
    Lie in dissevered beds of dreamless sleep—
Oh! would that here the marble I might raise
    Above their dust, and sorrow's vigil keep;
The corse bring hither from the distant West
Of one I loved the best.

## IV.

She lies too near the crowded thoroughfare,
    And rattling wheels throw dust upon her tomb;
She loved the mountain, and the liberal air—
    Spring's violet beauty, and rich summer's bloom
Ah! more of peace would harbor in my breast
Could here that loved one rest.

## V.

And she of winning look and sunny tress,
    Of softly rounded cheek and dark-blue eye—
My long-mourned daughter, lovely little Bess,
    Cut off untimely, by her side should lie;
Yon brook that sends its murmur to mine ear
Speaks of those dead ones dear.

## VI.

Here death arrays his form in softest guise,
  And Beauty, stricken by his mortal blow,
Who comes with folded arms and curtained eyes,
  He welcomes with a lover's whisper low;
And perished childhood, with a smiling face,
Folds in his hushed embrace.

## VII.

Ambition, here, his struggles, dreams and hopes
  All ended, like a child may lay him down—
The flitting shadow on yon mountain slopes,
  Apt symbol of his dream of wild renown:
And Pleasure, sated with life's wasting wine,
Her head in peace recline.

## VIII.

These hillocks, swelling over silent breasts,
  Seem waves of life arrested in their flow,
And a deep calm, as of Elysium, rests
  On upland ridge and glen that lies below,
And first, beneath the light of vernal skies,
Here violets uprise.

## IX.

Sweet Place of Graves! I thank thee for the calm
  Thy landscape has infused into my soul—
The wounded bosom here may find a balm,
  And life grow tranquil as it nears the goal;
This scene, composed of forest, wave and hill,
Makes the wild pulse grow still,

## MEMORIAL LINES

INSCRIBED TO BEREAVED PARENTS.

I.

What precious balm can song impart
To lessen woe that parents bear,
When throbs no more the gentle heart
Of one so gifted, good and fair!
The feathered harbingers of May
Revisit northern haunts again,
While school mates listen to their lay,
But, ah! for her they chant in vain.

II.

We know that breaking is the light
Round her, of Heaven's eternal dawn,
And that unknown are death and night
Where one so pure as she hath gone;
That better is a land of bliss
For spirits of celestial mould;
But, full of agony, we miss
The face that cheered us to behold.

III.

Long lashes shaded eyes of blue
From which looked forth a soul of love,
Deep as midsummer skies in hue
When not a cloud is seen above;
Soft hair, as with a halo, crowned
Her head and gleamed like golden ore;
Those wond'rous locks, in song renowned,
Less bright that Petrarch's Laura wore.

### IN.

Ah! what hath been no more can be,
　For early was her requiem sung;
The youngest of our flock was she,
　And favorite of old and young.
We miss her footfall on the stair,
　Her kiss of welcome at the door,
And tells a tale, yon vacant chair,
　Of beauty flown forevermore.

### V.

Our darling of the radiant curls
　Dwells where Omniscience claims his own,
For caskets that enclose such pearls
　Are wedded to the dust alone.
Lost lamb! with life's brief conflict tired,
　On the Good Shepherd's tender breast
Sleep, while we breathe those words inspired,
　"He giveth his beloved rest."

## BURIAL OF BIRDIE.

### I.

It was meet that one so sweet
　Should be drest in bridal white
When her heart had ceased to beat,
　And her orbs had closed in night.

Flowers were in her little hand,
  And like one asleep she lay
While a pale and sorrowing band
  Wept for Beauty passed away.

II.

It was meet that one so sweet,
  Dead should wear the robes of life,
Not the ghastly winding sheet
  Making death with terror rife.
Golden brown the silken hair
  On the rounded temples fell,
And like work of sculptor rare
  Was the face we loved so well.

III.

It was meet that one so sweet
  From the war of life should flee,
'And with golden-sandaled feet
  Walk where roars no angry sea.
Dead? our Birdie is not dead!
  In that box lies beauteous clay,
But her cherub soul hath fled
  To the Land of Light away.

IV.

It is meet that dust so sweet
  Should in May be laid to rest,
And that form with grace replete,
  In a stainless garb be drest.
With a longing in her heart
  For her Heavenly Father's fold,
She was destined to depart
  Early from a clime so cold.

### V.

It is meet that one so sweet,
   Loaned to dark earth for a day,
Back to Heaven, her native seat,
   Like a bird should wing her way. `
Let no dismal dirge be sung,
   No chill ritual be read,
When the beautiful and young
   To their Father's House have fled.

### VI.

It was meet that one so sweet
   When she heard the Angels call
Should her mother's name repeat,
   And escape from mortal thrall.
Let this casket, doomed to waste,
   Gently to damp mould be given
While the jewel it encased
   Glitters in the crown of Heaven !

---

## CALLED AWAY.

### I.

Low, hollow murmurs from the clear southwest
   Announce the rolling of Spring's chariot wheels
Light dances on the mountain's stormy crest,
   And earth a rapture feels.

Those darlings, blue-eyed violets, ere long
   On the sour face of March will wake a smile,
While robin red-breast a rejoicing song
   Is warbling out the while.
The signs of resurrection are abroad
   After the wintry death-sleep of the flowers:
The chilly snow-paths that our feet have trod
   Will soften with warm showers:—

### II.

But, ah! early taken, the dead will not waken,
   Though hearts bleed and bitterly ache—
The shroud is around her and fetters have bound her
   That conquering Spring cannot break:
Young March is not bringer of life to the singer
   Whose wood-notes were warbled so well:
A charmed lute is broken, the last word is spoken,
   And, hark! to yon death-tolling bell!

### III.

I hear a voice that thus rebukes complaint—
   "The grave can set no bounds to buried worth,
Only clay garments an ascended saint
   Leaves to cold, covering earth."
No lines of care her face will darken more,
   No bitter pang shoot through her trembling form;
Won is the crown, for well the cross she bore
   Through darkness, grief and storm.
She is not dead—to give her welcome grand
   Blest lyres to notes of jubilee were strung
When through the golden gates of Morning Land
   She passed, pure, radiant, young."

Though, wild grief controlling, such words are con
    soling
When the lovely grow wan and take leave,
For sweet, vanished faces and drear, vacant places
    The heart that is coldest must grieve ;
And one has departed—a minstrel true-hearted—
    Whose strain, like the nightingale's lay,
Though dark the sky o'er us, cheered gloom with its
    chorus
    While doubt and dread vanished away.

-----

## MEMORIAL LINES.

### I.

Again the moon of bursting flowers
    Decks like a bride the landscape fair ;
How jubilant the fall of showers—
    How full of balm the bracing air !
But night-clouds on my soul descend,
    Though outward nature is aglow,
While thinking of a youthful friend
    Who perished one brief year ago.

### II.

Commanding view of wood and wave,
    Broad level mead and breezy hill,
I stood beside the verdant grave
    Where slept his ashes hushed and still ;

And musing there I deemed a spot
　　So picturesque, retired and sweet,
Where blossoms breathed " forget him not,"
　　Had hallowed been by angel feet.

### III.

I doubt not that a martyr's crown
　　He wears amidst the Heavenly Host,
By fearful accident cut down
　　While braving death at Duty's post.
O stricken father ! mourn no more !
　　The mystic river he has crossed,
And sainted ones upon the shore
　　Have crowned thy boy, too early lost.

### IV.

Though sailing on a troubled sea,
　　The blissful port of peace is near,
And promises vouchsafed to thee
　　A Christian mariner should cheer.
There will the parted meet again,
　　Hand clasped to hand and face to face,
Thy noble boy, bewailed in vain,
　　With clasping arms thy neck embrace.

---

## A REMEMBRANCE.

### I.

The grapes hang blue upon the frame,
　　The peach is blushing on the bough ;

The sunset with a golden flame
  Has tipped the western mountain's brow;
September wears the look he wore
  When sorely were my heart-strings tried—
When gloom was thrown the landscape o'er,
    And Bessie died.

II.

The sad gray years are thrust between
  The poet and that mournful hour
When in her loveliness was seen
  My darling dead in home's sweet bower;
But fresh in my remembrance still,
    Though sons have fallen at my side,
Is that dark hour of gloom and ill
    When Bessie died.

III.

She was a child of softest bloom,
  Too fair for this dark land of shade,
And through the portals of the tomb
  She passed in angel-robes arrayed.
Like bright September's sun-set cloud
  Her rounded cheek and lips were dyed;
For me no terror hath the shroud
    Since Bessie died.

IV.

Ere closed her second year I heard
  The summons of the Mower, death,
And hushed was home's bright singing bird
  When drawn was her last fluttering breath.

The day was clear and bright like this,
　But she expired ere eventide ;
I lost all trust in mortal bliss
　When Bessie died.

### v.

Since that dread hour a noble boy
　Has in the battle's front been slain ;
Another, full of hope and joy,
　Drowned, never to revive again ;
But darkest was that hour of woe,
　Most sorely was the poet tried
When, like a wreath of melting snow,
　His Bessie died.

---

## THE ANNIVERSARY.

*"Graves are but the footsteps of the angel of eternal life."*
JEAN PAUL.

### I.

May laughs, dropping dew from her tresses,
　For the reign of the Frost King is o'er ;
Blue-eyed, like our lost one, she dresses
　The grave where she slumbers once more.
The lark unmolested is building
　Amidst hiding grasses her nest,
And bright dandelions are gilding
　The green plaid that covers her breast.

## II.

Like flute notes that melt in the distance,
  Her last song hath died on the ear ;
Though ended brief mortal existence,
  She dwells in a happier sphere.
Unfit for this valley of sorrow
  Are beings so fragile and fair ;
Though present to-day, on the morrow
  To the Isles of the Blest they repair.

## III.

The mirth of the household was ended
  When dying she lay without moan,
And May-time grew dark when descended
  A blight on our rose-bud half blown.
Our blossom too early that perished,
  Torn rudely from home's ravaged bower,
By soft airs of Paradise nourished
  Hath opened its leaves in full flower.

## IV.

Fled away when the season was vernal
  Our waif from a Heavenly shore ;
Tired of play, on the bosom maternal
  Her head she will pillow no more.
The garland is dust that once bound it,
  And changed is its contour to mould ;
One curl of the many that crowned it
  Alone emits lustre like gold.

## V.

Last eve, by the light of stars roaming,
  I felt that her spirit was nigh,

And a voice, in the hush of the gloaming,
   Made thus to my quest low reply :
" Drear thoughts of the charnel-house banish,
   Hearse, coffin and mouldering urn :
From sight, though the beautiful vanish,
   Sometimes they have leave to return."

## THE DYING SAINT.

### I.

Pass on to rest and victory,
   Tried champion of the Cross !
Although thy everlasting gain
   Is our embittered loss.
The waves of mortal life subside
   Upon the shores of time,
And death ere long on changing clay
   Will set his seal sublime.

### II.

Mother in Israel ! we know
   There is in store for thee
A crown that fadeth not away,
   Beyond the troubled sea ;
There will thy husband, gone before,
   His aged partner greet,
And in a house not made with hands
   Love's scattered household meet:

### III.

Guide of my youth and riper age,
  Beloved by me and mine,
The beauty of a cloudless eve
  Lends grace to thy decline.
Oh ! death-bed of the good and just !
  I never shall forget
Friends gathering like stars around
  A sun about to set.

### IV

Intelligence survived the power
  To utter parting words,
And sweetly on her listening ear
  Fell notes of summer birds ;
I felt her gently clasping hand,
  Although she could not speak,
And light, as from the Better Land,
  Fell on her pale, thin cheek.

### V.

The low, balm-breathing air of June
  Stole through the open door,
But could not to the wasted face
  Its roses lost restore ;
Though o'er it an expression came
  More beautiful than bloom,
A signal that the passing soul
  Had conquered grief and gloom.

### VI.

Alas ! my pen is uninspired
  In fitting words to paint

The closing of a righteous life,
  The death-bed of a saint.
The gates of glory ope for her,
  Then why deplore our loss?
Pass on to rest and victory,
  Tried champion of the Cross!

# Songs & Ballads

# THE PINE.

## I.

WHILE mossy old pines sang a lullaby wild,
   I couched on the grass, when an innocent child,
    And fancied that angels were hovering round ;
No instrument fashioned by frail mortal hand
Could rouse in my bosom a feeling so grand
    As that magical, soft and mysterious sound.

## II.

In keeping with Freedom's proud throne on the hills,
How the roar of a storm-troubled pine forest thrills
    The heart of the mountaineer mantled in cloud ;
It sends to the valleys a voice of dismay,
And sounds like the quick march of hosts to the fray,
    While drums beat the charge and the trumpet is loud.

## III.

Though soft are the tones that the wild winds evoke
From the glossy-leaved beech or centennial oak,
    The pines give a sweeter response to their call ;
And often I think, when the branches are stirred,
Of rich, organ peals in some old minster heard,
    While ghosts seem to start from the echoing wall.

## IV.

When winter is coating the hillside with snow,
And dropping a shroud on the meadows below,

The pine, like a sentinel, stands on the height ;
Ice covers its trunk with a glittering mail,
And it welcomes the rush of the pitiless gale,
   Its green arms uptossing in frantic delight.

### V.

Meet place for the bird of our banner to rest,
Or build for his royal descendant a nest,
   Is the tall, misty cone of some towering pine ;
Its branches give tongue and proclaim him a king
When sunward, in circles, he mounts on the wing,
   To gaze on the earth like a vision divine.

### VI.

Oh ! grand is the dash of the surf on the shore,
And wild the mad torrent's tumultuous roar,
   While cliffs overhanging with spray-drops are wet ;
But the sigh of the wind in a forest of pines,
Like troops on the hill-summits, marshalled in lines,
   Is a sound that a poet can never forget.

### VII.

Now it swells on the ear, with a billowy roll ;
Anon breathes in whispers of love to the soul—
   For spirits are touching the emerald keys :
Talk not of the magic of lute or of lyre,
Poetic emotion they cannot inspire
   Like melody woke in the pines by the breeze.

## WHAT I WOULD BE.

### I.

What would I be?   Not rich in gold
  And with a narrow heart,
Or, misanthropic, stern and cold,
  Dwell from my kind apart?
I would not be a man of war,
  Who looks on death unmoved,
Give me a title dearer far:
  "The well-beloved!"

### II.

I would not wear a laurel crown,
  Its leaves conceal the thorn ;
Too oft the children of renown
  Are friendless and forlorn.
Oh ! let me lead a blameless life,
  By young and old approved ;
Called, in a world of sin and strife,
  " The well beloved !"

### III.

God grant me power to guard the weak,
  And sorrow's moaning hush,
And never feel upon my cheek
  Dark Shame's betraying blush ;
And when at my creator's call
  From earth I am removed,
Let Friendship 'broider on my pall :
  " The well beloved !"

## BLUE-EYED FLORENCE.

#### I.

Blue-Eyed Florence! where art thou
With thy radiant baby-brow,
And thy voice of silvery tone,
And thy smile, an angel's own?
Place upon thy father's knee
Well I know was dear to thee ;
He is toiling far away,
And hath vanished many a day
Since he crossed home's cottage sill—
Is his love remembered still?

#### II.

Blue-eyed Florence, it was bliss
Every morn to claim thy kiss,
Feel from this world-weary heart
Dross and earthiness depart—
Sharer in thy love—so bright
With a flash of heavenly light—
Listen, while thy mother smiled,
To thy questions, darling child !
Puzzling to the wisest brain—
Will that bliss return again?

#### III.

Brightest of the rosy band
In sweet childhood's fairy land,
Does remembrance ever stray
To thy father, far away?

Dost thou, when a thought of him
Comes thy sunny joy to dim,
Sometimes, with a moistening eye,
Throw thy doll and play-things by?
Is his name upon thy tongue
When the matin hymn is sung!

### IV.

Blue-eyed Florence! when I meet
Little children in the street,
Closely do I hunt for traces
Of thy beauty in their faces;
For thy burst of joy unbounded,
For thy temples fair and rounded,
For thy glance of star-like beam,
And thy hair of golden gleam;
For thy motion like a linnet,
And thy laugh with music in it,
And I bless them if I find
Aught recalling thee to mind.

### V.

Ah! it is a grievous wrong
We should parted be so long;
That thy carol, like a bird,
Must by other ears be heard,
Singing some quaint nursery air
In thy little rocking chair;
Others mark thy budding charms—
Others toss thee in their arms,
While thy father, sad and lonely,
Sees thee in a night-dream only.

## THINGS COMING.

### I.

Morn is coming ;—hear the lark !
Rose-streaks in the orient mark !
Earth will soon be fair to view
Like a Beauty bathed in dew.

### II.

Night is coming—holy night !
Stars her arching dome will light,
And the moon, with silver horn,
Travel on to meet the morn.

### III.

Joy is coming—light of tread,
With a wreath-encircled head ;
Brief, but sweet will be his stay
Ere he vanishes away.

### IV.

Grief is coming—on the gale
Soon will float her sable veil,
Strewing, while she wildly grieves,
Funeral earth with cypress leaves.

### V.

Spring is coming—vernal rains
Soon will warm Earth's frozen veins,
And the violets will rise
Tinted with cerulean dyes.

### VI.

Summer 's coming—in the wave
Wing-tips will the swallow lave,
And the blossoms that unclose
Will out-blush the sunset's rose.

### VII.

Autumn 's coming—with his frost
Blighting flowers, the early lost !
Blackening each fragile stem,—
Vainly will we mourn for them.

### VIII.

Winter 's coming, and our feet
Soon will soil his winding sheet ;
Iced in armor, he will hear
Our appeal with deafened ear.

### IX.

Death is coming — for no prayer
Will the ghostly king forbear ;
In his fleshless arms to fold
Rich and poor, the young and old.

### X.

When the Reaper comes to reap
Let us fold our arms in sleep,
Trusting that a God of love
Will our spirits waft above.

## THINGS FLYING.

### I.

Time is flying—fast the sand
Leaves the hour-glass in his hand;
Where his feet have hurried by
Ashes, bones and ruins lie.

### II.

Hope is flying—this her strain,
While she seeks the open main,
" Where the waters foam and rage,
I can find no anchorage."

### III.

Ah ! the star is fading fast
That burned bright above her mast,
And the midnight soon will veil
Her bright, disappearing sail.

### IV.

Peace is flying—notes of war,
Trumpet, drum, and cannon-jar
Have affrighted her from earth,
And she seeks her place of birth.

### V.

Birds are flying—Autumn drear
Whispers of old Winter near,
And they seek the golden strand
Of some flowery tropic land.

### VI.

Leaves are flying, sere and pale,
On the wild November gale;
Thus poor human glory flies,
Thus dissolve our earthly ties.

### VII.

Youth is flying—and his voice
Will the heart no more rejoice;
On his bloom hath fallen blight,
Changing it to corpse-like white.

### VIII.

Love is flying—woe and sin
Have our Eden entered in;
Funeral dirge and tolling bell
Marred the song he sang so well.

### IX.

Wealth is flying—let it fly!
Trust in things that cannot die;
Coffins, destined for the mould,
Vainly we inlay with gold.

### X.

Truth is flying—weary strife
He hath waged with wrong for life;
Armed again for conflict stern,
Let us pray for his return!

### XI.

Pray that God may give him power
In the deadly trial-hour;
While the hosts of sin and error
At his war-cry flee in terror.

## TASSO'S FAREWELL.

### I.

I will never cease to love thee,
While the stars keep watch above me;
In thy laugh is music ringing,
And thy voice is sweet in singing;
Love-light, in thy bright eye beaming,
Wakes the poet from his dreaming,
And thy smile hath summer in it,
But that heart—would I could win it!

### II.

Tell me, tell me by what token
Can I prove my vow unbroken
When my soul, with rapture burning,
Counts the hours of my returning,
After absence long and dreary,
Toiling through the winter weary,
To regain the wreath that crowned me,
Ere the bonds of evil bound me.

### III.

When my day of storm is ended,
If my soul hath not ascended,
I will come to thee in vision
From my happy home Elysian,
Cheer thee in thine hours despairing,
Guard thee, for thy welfare caring,
Knowing, when this life is over,
Thou in Heaven wilt meet thy lover.

IV.

'Till extinguished life's last ember,
Leonor I will remember,
Though the cruel fates dissever
Those who should be ONE forever;
I will see my love in dreaming,
Think of her when morn is beaming,
And her name shall live in story,
Woven in my crown of glory.

## SONG.

I.

When will this heartache cease,
  Ruin before me;
When will the Dove of Peace
  Spread his wing o'er me?
Far from "this shoal of time,"
  Stranger to sorrow,
Will not some brighter clime
  Bid me good morrow!
      Raven's croak:
"Trust not to-morrow!"

II.

Fame has a phantom proved
  Worth not the chasing;
Lost ones, the well beloved,
  Earth is embracing:

On the dear household hearth
  Not a spark flashes;
Where rang the voice of mirth,
  Cold lie the ashes:
        Raven's croak:
"All dust and ashes!"

### III.

How can the eagle soar,
  Broken his pinion?
King he will rule no more
  Air's blue dominion:
How can the minstrel sing
  With his doom written,
By Despair's mortal sting
  Fearfully smitten —
        Raven's croak:
"Fearfully smitten!"

### IV.

Hark! from the clouds above
  Voices are calling
"Trust to Eternal Love,
  Though night is falling;
Daylight will break at last,
  Darkness will vanish;
Thoughts of the mournful Past
  From your soul banish—
        Angels cry
"From your soul banish!"

## MY DAUGHTERS.

### I.

What flowers are meet for me so sweet
  As my daughter, eldest born?
A violet crown the glossy brown
  Of her locks would best adorn.
When the lines I trace of her gentle face,
  I think an angel near;
And griefs that sting my heart take wing
  Her lute-like voice to hear.

### II.

I will twine a wreath of the mountain heath
  For my youngest daughter's brow;
For her well tuned ear delights to hear
  The wind in the pine tree's bough.
Six summers bright a golden light
  On her clustering curls have shed,
And I feel the glow of long ago,
  When I list to her bounding tread.

### III.

Her soul has fire that says "aspire!"
  Let good or ill betide;
And her gleesome call is like the fall
  Of streams down a mountain's side.
Long lashes fringe, with a darkening tinge,
  Eyes blue as the Alpine flower;
And in her glance burns wild romance,
  Boon Nature's fearful dower.

#### IV.

For the brow of my third, that radiant bird,
　　What chaplet shall I weave—
My spirit child, that a moment smiled,
　　And of guilty earth took leave?
For her fair young brow, angelic now,
　　Twine amaranthine flowers;
In the land of light, with the blest and bright,
　　She walks through thornless bowers.

#### V.

This golden tress of little Bess,
　　Remembrance wildly wakes;
On her infant cheek was the roseate streak
　　When a bright June morning breaks.
They say she died and, where tears are dried,
　　That she walks in endless youth;
That her spirit near her father dear
　　Whispers the words of truth.

---

## A FRIEND'S WISHES.

#### I.

I wish you joy and health, my boy!
　　A purse with gold well lined;
To bless thy life, a virtuous wife
　　Of cultivated mind!

May peace attend thy cruise, my friend !
  Down life's swift rolling stream;
No cloud on high to rob thy sky
  Of sunlight's cheerful gleam.

### II.

May age to thee no winter be,
  But like the summer glow;
And song and fame light up a flame
  Beneath thy locks of snow:
And Heaven thy soul, when reached time's goal,
  Receive within its bowers,
To meet once more friends gone before,
  Crowned with unwithering flowers.

## AN ÆOLIAN MELODY.

### I.

My bosom has Æolian cords,
  That warble wildly to the soul,
And oft the strain takes form in words
  That echo like a death-bell's toll;
Anon it makes my pulses beat
With power beyond expression sweet,

### II.

The door of my sad heart it opes,
  And memories wake long cold and dead;

The ashes of a thousand hopes
  Stir in their dark and mouldering bed—
Loved faces, in that heart enshrined,
Bring back the mournful Past to mind.

### III.

Unearthly songs that long have slept,
  To chant defying mortal skill
Wake, when those bosom chords are swept
  That soon will broken be, and still.
Alas ! those chords, though finely strung,
Can never sing as they have sung.

### IV.

Long have I walked beneath a cloud,
  The seal of doom upon my brow !
Off with these laurel wreaths ! the shroud
  Would best become the mortal now ;
For one, long-loved, cannot be mine—
I stained with guilt—she half-divine.

### V.

These bosom-chords in happier days,
  To joyous melodies kept time,
But now, attuned to saddest lays,
  Alone with wailing voices chime ;
Or make Æolian reply
To a lost soul's despairing cry.

## GREETING TO MARY.

### I.

Happy New-Year! to Mary dear,
   From one whose heart is aching;
Her image fair is painted there
   Although its chords are breaking.
May saints keep guard, my Mary ward
   From ills to life belonging;
And on her way, from day to day,
   May angel guides be thronging,
     In hours of deep dejection,
     To give her hope, protection.

### II.

While New-Year chimes revive old times,
   Though full of solemn warning,
Wake, harp-strings wake, the silence break,
   And give my love good morning!
May nought annoy, the birds of joy
   Sing in her praise forever;
The demon Care, the ghoul, Despair,
   Molest my Mary never,
     While Heaven at last receives her—
     A crown of glory weaves her.

## MY SCOTTISH BEAUTIES.

### I.

Ellen, Jean and Flora
   I prize all things above,
With blushes like Aurora,
   Smiles like the Queen of Love.
They are my own three Graces
   With eyes that flash delight,
May Time on their sweet faces
   One wrinkle never write.

### II.

Thy form, majestic Ellen!
   Thy proud and stately mien
Should grace no humbler dwelling
   Than palace of a Queen.
Across the dark blue water,
   In Europe's ancient land
Was never born a daughter
   With air of more command.

### III.

I know that there are many
   More dazzling in their charms,
But Burns would long, sweet Jenny!
   To clasp you in his arms.
When near I feel devotion
   As if thou wert a shrine—
Eyes, with the blue of ocean
   In their clear depths, are thine.

### IV.

And Flora, gentle Flora,
   Unsung thou shalt not be;
Rose, Mary, Blanche and Cora
   Are names less dear to me.
Thy household virtues make thee
   A wife to be desired;
For life the bard would take thee
   Although in rags attired.

### V.

I am no pleasure-seeker,
   A sober life I live,
But fill, fill high the beaker,
   And pledge the toast I give!
"Ellen, Jean and Flora
   I prize all things above,
With blushes like Aurora,
   Smiles like the Queen of Love."

---

## SNOW FLAKE AND ONNOLEE.

### I.

There is a mare whose silken hair
   Gleams in the sun like gold,
Her nostrils spread and beauteous head
   Show lineage high and bold.

Blood, speed and bone will make her known
    Wherever reins are drawn;
Like other steeds no whip she needs
    To swiftly urge her on.

### II.

And by her side, with even stride,
    Speeds Onnolee, her mate;
The bits she champs while on she tramps
    Untiring in her gait.
The look of game in her sinewy frame
    Commands the turfmen's praise;
On her glossy coat and mane afloat
    The ladies' love to gaze.

### III.

An Arab sire has given fire
    To dark eyes full and clear;
Away with checks for their arching necks
    While both outpace the deer!
The fastest nag in rear must lag
    When they are stripped to trot;
Though bad the track they will not slack,
    Of a breed that falters not.

### IV.

Sure-footed, strong, they move along
    Fleet as the gliding doe;
Hooves small and round upon the ground
    Fall light as flakes of snow.
Each agile limb of these trotters trim
    Is laced with swelling veins:
Look out! look out! when they're about,
    And Harry holds the reins!

## " INSULA SANCTORUM."

### I.

If souls were free from fraud and guile,
    And ignorance had less effrontery;
If battle blades were sheathless while
    One traitor lived to curse his country;
If far more prized than golden ore
    At Freedom's shrine were deep devotion,
The sainted Isle would flash once more,
    A jewel on the breast of ocean.

### II.

When ages of Oppression rest
    Upon a land once bright with glory—
Resentment in each generous breast
    Enkindled by her mournful story—
Better the cannon's angry peal
    To rouse than tongue that idly preaches—
The ringing rhetoric of steel
    Than eloquence of uttered speeches.

### III.

When Valor finds in danger's hour
    The mask of Honor worn by Treason,
And thrown away on lawless Power
    Are arguments though based on reason,
Resolve to win the field, or die,
    Should waken as one man the Nation,
While bugle call and rallying cry
    Are heard, not empty declamation.

IV

If hearts to dare and heads to plan
   In crushing tyranny united,
Then in his majesty would man
   Rise up, and every wrong be righted;
If men would ancient feuds forego,
   And faction cease to make commotion,
Outshining moon again would glow
   Our Emerald on the breast of Ocean.

## LONGING FOR SUMMER.

I.

How happy the swift birds of passage must be,
Flying southward in flocks over mainland and sea,
To rest their tired wings in some fair southern isle,
Where the bright eyes of summer eternally smile;
And thither, my love! had we wings we would fly,
Nevermore to live under this bleak northern sky!
Our forms are too frail and our hearts are too warm
For this desolate region of darkness and storm.

II.

Oh! long have I waited to rove, hand in hand,
With the girl of my heart in some tropical land;
We would banquet on fruitage, delicious and sweet,
While winds blowing landward would temper the
     heat,

And brilliant flamingoes, in scarlet arrayed,
Through the salt pools of ocean would sluggishly
      wade,
And birds, darting out from the cool leafy glooms,
The rainbow's own tints would flash back from their
      plumes.

### III.

I would build thee a home amidst whispering bowers,
While Time glided by, his old scythe wreathed with
      flowers;
I would hear in thine accents, unaided by art,
The music that passage would find to my heart,
And toil for thee only, my loved and my own!
In this drear world no longer heart-broken, alone;
No more looking mournfully into the past,
But, soul knit to soul, live and love to the last.

---

## SONG.

### I.

Bloom for us a little longer,
  Last Rose of the summer hours!
May your drooping stem grow stronger
  Kissed by silvery dew and showers.
The Flower-Queen gave a fragrant sigh,
Whispering with her sad good-bye!
  "Lonely, oh! so lonely!"

### II.

Last leaf of the forest clinging
    In the chill autumnal blast!
Listen to wild voices singing
    Of sweet things too bright to last;
Tongue the leaf in falling found
Singing with a rustling sound,
    " Lonely, oh ! so lonely ! "

### III.

Poet holding once communion
    With the forms of beauty flown,
Rent are golden cords of union,
    And thou wanderest alone :
Answered, pale and evil-starred,
With a wailing voice the Bard,
    " Lonely, oh ! so lonely ! "

### IV.

Let me cross the mystic river,
    Let me walk the radiant shore !
From the bonds of clay deliver
    One in love with earth no more :
Here, where fairest forms conceal
Oft such hollow heart, I feel
    " Lonely, oh ! so lonely ! "       .

## EASTER CAROL.

### I.

Rejoice thou that weepest,
  And hold up thy head;
Awake thou that sleepest—
  Arise from the dead!
Hope bursts from the prison
  That held her so long;
The shout—"Christ is risen!"
  Wakes earth into song.

### II.

Gross darkness is banished
  From Death's wintry cave,
And mourning has vanished
  Like mist from the wave;
For Christ light bestoweth,
  Though dark is the way,
The fount whence it floweth
  Is day—endless day.

### III.

Despair furls forever
  Her banner of gloom;
Its black fold will never
  Again wrap the tomb;
Hope bursts from the prison
  That held her so long;
The shout—"Christ is risen!"
  Wakes earth into song.

## ALONE.

### I.

In nevermore there is despair ;
  In fare-thee-well, a dirge-like tone ;
But agony, too hard to bear,
  Breathes in that mournful word—*alone!*
It tells of broken hearts and ties,
Long silent lips, and curtained eyes ;
Of vanished birds, abandoned nests,
And white hands clasped on silent breasts.

### II.

Alone ! alone ! what echoes wake
  In memory's cavern, at the sound ;
While phantoms their appearance make,
  As if the lost again were found.
But ah ! how desolate the thought
Such figures are of moonlight wrought :
Alone ! alone ! no sadder word
By mortal ear is ever heard.

## TO STELLA IN HEAVEN.

### I.

I have seen thee in my dreaming,
  I have though of thee by day,

And an eye on me is beaming ·
  In the distance far away.
The cloud that floats above me
  Takes the likeness of thy form;
Oh! say, dost thou still love me
  In a realm that knows not storm?

## II.

Where the crystal streams are rolling
  Through amaranthine bowers—
Unheard the death-bell tolling,
  As in this world of ours;
Where the form, divinely moulded,
  Is never laid to rest,
With the pale hands meekly folded
  On the frozen, pulseless breast.

## III.

Oh! say, dost thou remember
  When first I called thee mine,
Or quenched is love's bright ember
  In the home that now is thine?
The cloud that floats above me
  Takes the likeness of thy form,
Oh! say, dost thou still love me
  In a realm that knows not storm?

## JANE.

### I.

Far you must go, and look round you in vain
To find sweeter girl than my Highland lass, Jane;
Many be summers, with bird-notes and bowers,
That drop in her pathway their innocent flowers;
Ever, with Truth setting seal on her brow,
May she be pure, and as spotless as now !

### II.

In her blue eyes beams a soul-kindled light,
The lone star of eve is less placid and bright;
Tinged in her lip with the red of the dawn,
Light is her footstep as tread of the fawn;
Beauty has painted her cheek with the rose,
Round her a charm her own loveliness throws.

### III.

In the rich lines of that beautiful face,
Painter might find his true model of grace;
I know that her heart with affection is warm,
And sculptor might study the mould of her form:—
Far you must go and look around you in vain
To find fairer girl than my Highland lass, Jane.